Dedicated to my Dad – the first to read the first draft

©Copyright Geraldine Comiskey 2003

Front cover illustration ©Copyright Geraldine Comiskey

Geraldine Comiskey has asserted her right under the Copyright, Designs and Patents Act 1988 to be identified as the author of this work.

The moral right of the author has been asserted

A catalogue record for this book is available from the British Library

This book is a work of fiction and, except in the case of historical fact, any reference to actual persons, living or dead, actual events or locations, and the use of any names or characters, is purely coincidental.

Contents

Author's note	*5*
Characters	*6*
Map of Belgowan	*8*
Shampoo & Sympathy	
Roots	12
Regrowth	25
Highlights	30
Tints	34
Itchy scalp	40
Bigwigs	61
Getting tangled	68
Sticky gel	77
A hairy tale	81
Split ends	85
Dark grey roots	90
The chop	98
Dandruff	106
Extra-strong fixing gel	115

Acknowledgement	*121*
About the author	*122*
Other books	*123*
Reviews	*131*

Author's note:

The first draft of this book was written in the early 2000s. The world has changed tremendously since then: The Celtic Tiger has been and gone; everyone's circumstances have been affected by the pandemic, a worldwide migration crisis, the NATO war in Eurasia and massive shifts in social mores, work, social mores, science and technology.

When I wrote the first draft of this story, there was no social media (Bebo – remember that? – had yet to be born!); to watch a movie "on demand" you had to physically go to a video shop and rent a cassette the size of a brick; "reality TV" was just beginning, with the first season of Big Brother airing to a curious public; "identity politics" was something most of us in Europe, Ireland and Great Britain could barely imagine; the EU was merely an economic organisation – and not even in my wildest imagination could I have come up with the concept of multiple genders. Topics such as surrogacy were to be found only in niche literature and the success of movements such as Extinction Rebellion would only have been plausible in fantasy.

While I have made some changes to my original manuscript (which was typed on floppy discs), the story is still set in the Noughties, where its characters had to make do without Zoom, TikTok, WhatsApp, Shein and Tinder.

Characters

The stylists
Kay & Shay Duffy: a young couple, salon owners
Vicky Sheeran: their former boss, manager of a rival salon
Gary Wu: a renowned stylist
Sunita: a Spanish sex-bomb
Lorcan: a posh trainee
Roz: a beautician, Kay's best friend

The VIPs
Steve Oldman: lead singer of Jurassic Rox
Flash and Eric: Jurassic Rox drummer and bass guitarist
Giada: Eric's model wife
Andrew St John: famous orchestral conductor
Nit and Tick: Goth rockers
The Chainsaw Crucifixes: death metal band
Sniffa Dawg: Iconic rapper
Yo Yo Bling: Hip-hop legend
Neil Titwick: photographer for upmarket men's mag *Bloke*
Enrico Bendini: controversial Italian film director
Sylvie Fouton: French film icon
Mike Toopay: star of Seventies TV show *Cool Cops*
Rev Vernon Good: American televangelist
Stephanie Dunne: blockbuster author
George Morton: bestselling author of action thrillers
Linda Morton: George's cheating wife
Barbara Burrows: gossip columnist
Birgitta Stormberg: *Playboy* model
Willy Tighe: daytime TV host and election candidate
Dr Chad Wokeman: world authority on lesbian necrophiliacs
Dr Erika Slutzberger: marriage counsellor
Dr Rowena Edge: ex-nun, edgy feminist author
Dr Freudenstein: renowned psychotherapist
Dr McClone: fertility expert
Marina Wisebuy: ex-wife of a supermarket magnate
The Duchess of Straththigh: Catholic convert
Rasheed: yogi and spiritual guru

The locals:
Macker: fisherman & horror movie star
Maureen: Macker's wife & unofficial PA

Massimo: chipper, Macker's best customer
Fr Nick: starstruck parish priest
Muriel: church organist
Garda Sergeant Rory O'Reilly: veteran cop
Cllr Mickey Finn: veteran local representative
Cllr What's-his-name: one of the Venerable Grey Men
Jason Feeney: young upstart election candidate; Colin Farrell lookalike
Mustafa Bin Fahreg: wealthy immigrant and election candidate
Diarmuid "Keep Belgowan Common" O'Fogey: environmental campaigner
Sonny O'Toole: confirmed bachelor, election candidate
Sir Humphrey: West Brit election candidate
Elvis Fox: election candidate
Luigi Benvenuto: proprietor of Il Pasticcio restaurant
Charisse: glamorous boutique owner
Mrs Uberman: one of Belgowan's oldest and poshest residents
Moira: lead singer of local girl band
Anto Byrne: Mr O'Hare's drinking buddy
Mrs O'Toole: Kay & Shay's landlady, member of NAG (Neighbours Against Gays)
Mrs Finnerty: her friend and fellow member of NAG
Mrs Keegan: Sunita's landlady, proud mother of champion Irish dancers
Pierre: Linda Morton's personal trainer
Javier: Linda Morton's horse-riding instructor
Marco: the Mortons' chef
Gouger: local bailiff
Hobbler: protection racket boss
Mr Cramp: bank manager

Outsiders:
Suzy Mata: Linda Morton's estranged sister, restauranteur
Brad Fisher: American lawyer
Witch & cowboy: dole queue veterans

The folks:
Mr & Mrs O'Hare: Kay's parents
Geraldine: Kay's aunt, fortune-teller
Sharon: Shay's aunt
Barry: Shay's brother
Bernie & Starsky: Kay's siblings
Fergal: Bernie's boyfriend
Robbie: Bernie & Fergal's little boy
Vidal: Kay & Shay's dog

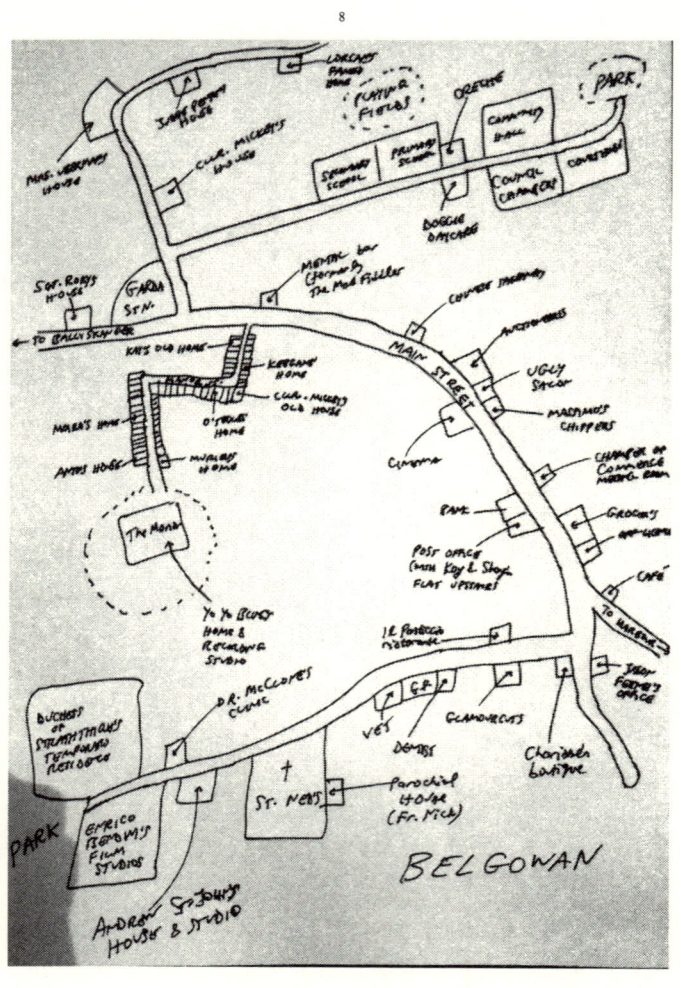

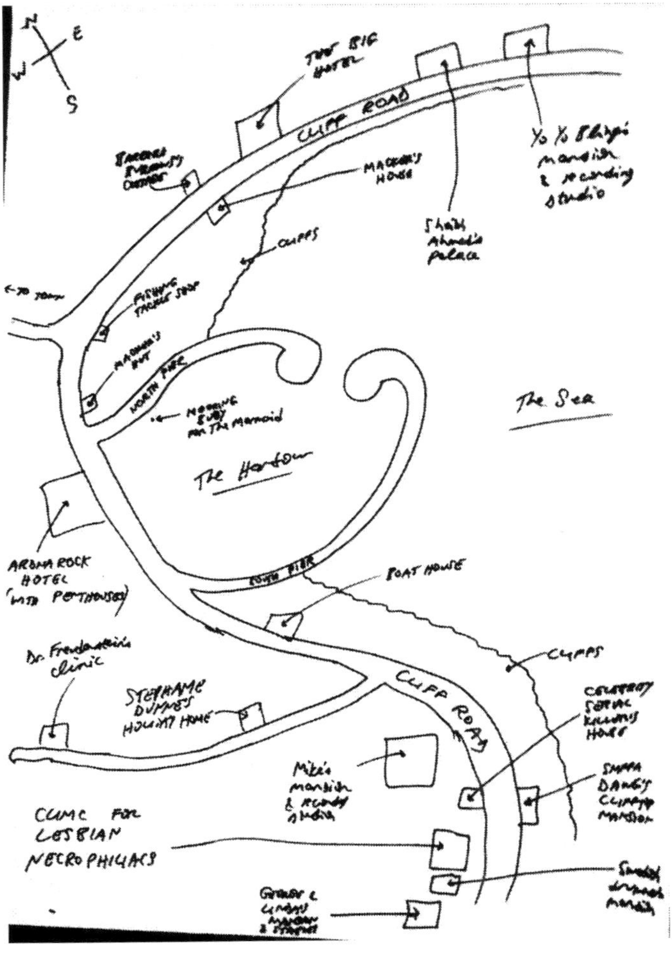
N
E
W
S
THE BIG HOTEL
CLIFF ROAD
CLIFFS
← TO TOWN
FISHING TACKLE SHOP
NORTH PIER
MOORING BUOY
for the mermaid
The Sea
The Harbour
ARONA ROCK HOTEL
(WITH PENTHOUSES)
SOUTH PIER
BOAT HOUSE
CLIFFS
STEPHANIE DUNNE'S HOLIDAY HOME
CLIFF ROAD
Mike's mansion & recording studio
CLINIC FOR LESBIAN NECROPHILIACS

10

Shampoo & Sympathy

By Geraldine Comiskey

Roots

How could we have known what was going on inside George Morton's head? 'We're hairdressers, not bleedin headshrinks', as Shay said at the time.

But when George confessed to murder, we knew he wasn't joking. After all, he doesn't write comedy – and his violent thrillers are supposed to be based on in-depth research.

There was no mystery about why he told us; everyone confides in hairdressers. Still, there's no such thing as idle chat in this town. And our own story is a hairy tale.

I suppose you could call us 'disadvantaged', Shay and me. That's how we probably appear to our clients, who are all dead posh, stinking rich – or just pretending to be.

Our hairdressing salon is located here in Dublin's poshest suburb, a little coastal town called Belgowan. It used to be a fishing port but, these days, the only trawling done is for compliments, the blokes working the nets are all software zillionaires and the hookers won't get into bed for less than ten thousand (per head at an orgy). Belgowan is the place for people who've been everywhere, done everyone worth knowing, are paid a fortune to wear a T-shirt – and even more for taking it off. You see, this is Ireland's answer to the Riviera – the special-edition, totally cool sunless version.

It was a name-dropper's heaven long before the "boom" – and still is. It's as if the Recession never happened. Rock and film stars, TV presenters, snooker players, the idle heirs to family fortunes, polo-playing tycoons, the man who owns your local supermarket (whether you live in Dublin or Marbella), major drug-dealers and the people who make films about them, celebrity couples and the lawyers who divorce them, playboys, toyboys.... They all move here to live.

Our neighbours are so famous they don't need a mention in *Who's Who*; they're 'You Know Who'. These are the people who turn down offers by *Hello* magazine to have their weddings paid for because they don't need the publicity – or because it's the last thing they need. They move here to hide – from tax officials all over the world, grasping families and hangers-on, fans, stalkers, people who ask too many questions.

You might think this is the worst place to live. The town is crawling with social climbers who have moved here just for the privilege of sending their toddlers to the same crèche as some unsuspecting film star's kid, to be thumped in the school playground by the son of a professional boxer, to compete in the local beauty contest alongside the daughter of a supermodel, or to go through rebellious adolescence with the son of a Hollywood hellraiser.

PTA meetings are packed with middle-class mums and dads who feel inferior as the school principal fawns over some hard-rockin heavy-metal legend who turns up in ripped leather jeans, a graffitied T-shirt, a studded collar – and more studs pierced in his eyebrows than David Beckham's boots.

High society here often means just that.

But the amazing thing about Belgowan – and about Ireland as a whole – is that it doesn't attract the sleazy stalkers who hang around Hollywood and Monte Carlo (for one thing, anyone in chain-store sneakers would be stared into embarrassment here).

Don't get me wrong: Ireland is as fame-obsessed as any country. We buy *Hello* and *The National Enquirer*, and our national papers are full of celebrity scandal – even the broadsheets – but we wouldn't be caught dead asking for an autograph or taking a photo of a famous person. We're too cool – and, as our local Z-listers are always reminding us, we're too begrudging. The typical Irish reaction to success is: 'Who does that plonker think he is with his fancy car and his anorexic wife?'

So a VIP can safely jog down the park with no make-up, greasy hair and his granny's thermal knickers over a pair of leggings, and your man on the street will just say: 'Ah, that must be what's-his-face Christopher Reeve practising for a comeback – Jayz, fair play to him! Isn't he supposed to be dead?' – and no one will call the papers. Not that the papers will give a tinker's curse, if there's no sex involved.

The only thing more important in Ireland than sex is the drink. Even the European paparazzi who occasionally come over here get distracted by the Irish pub culture and forget all about their prey.

So the only stalkers you'll find in Ireland – and especially in Belgowan – are lower-middle-class groupies whose parents re-mortgaged the family home to send them to Swiss finishing school and ballet lessons; the kind of educated girls who are able to read magazines such as *Forbes* and the *Financial Times* in the original language (I'd need a tabloid translation).

These girls know what they're looking for and how to get him – and, because that usually involves a high-maintenance hairstyle, they come into our salon every two weeks.

So how, you might ask, did two ordinary people like Shay and myself get to open a hair salon here at the age of 24 – when the Celtic Tiger was in full roar? Well, I was born in this town, back in 1979, before it was fashionable (my sister Bernie always says we brought a bit of glamour to it and changed it forever). I grew up in a two-storey, two-bedroomed council house in a little terrace off the main street (which is called Manor Street, even though there's only one manor on it and most of the other buildings are shops – but I suppose 'Shop Street' wouldn't be posh enough for a town like this).

My parents used to rent the house off the council – for the kind of money that, these days, wouldn't even get you a cappuccino in one of the elegant cafés around here.

Then, when I was seven, Dad got off unemployment assistance and 'onto the pig's back', as Mam described it, meaning he was in luck: he got a permanent, pensionable job as a road sweeper with the council, thanks to our old friend, Councillor Mickey Finn (who, by way of payment, expects Dad to buy him a pint every time he sees him).

But my Dad landed on the pig's back*side*, because, along with the new job, he lost his right to taxpayer-subsidised rental accommodation. So we all moved to Ballyskanger, a huge suburb on Dublin's western periphery, way out past the traffic-blocked wasteland of Clonbollard…and far away from Belgowan with its little coves and its fishermen's boats, its cosy pubs and our nosey neighbours who would always give you a cup of milk if the shops were closed and would help with all family crises, whether it meant babysitting Bernie and me, stomach-pumping our big brother, Starsky, after he OD-ed on e-tabs or waking out my granny on the kitchen table because we wanted to respect her lifelong fear of undertakers.

Now Dad had to get two buses to sweep the streets of Belgowan every morning, Mam had to take out a loan to buy a little car so she could go to the shopping mall, Starsky had to find a local dealer and go through the usual initiation rites (he had to rob a few video shops just to prove he wasn't a cop because his accent sounded 'country' in Ballyskanger) – and Bernie and I had to play in our tiny back garden because Mam was afraid we'd get run over by lorries or kidnapped by men in white vans on the big motorway at the back of the house.

A few years later, the council started allowing its tenants to buy the houses at a subsidised rate. Many did – and sold them for a fortune to the yuppie speculators who were planning to make an even bigger profit by reselling them to tax-exiles.

I was fifteen and wearing a St Fiacla's school uniform when the lead singer from Jurassic Rox bought himself a mansion on the cliffs in Belgowan. I would have been his neighbour – and he loved girls in school uniforms, according to the tabloid which broke the news.

Right then, in front of all my classmates, I swore to return to Belgowan. 'You'll have to go for elocution lessons and pretend that your dad's a tax-dodger or that your brother's a major drug-dealer', my best friend Roz pointed out. 'Then you'll have to fall on a wet floor in a supermarket to get an insurance claim that will pay for a mouthful of crowns and designer clothes.'

But I was setting my sights higher than purgatory in an estate agent's office or a PR firm, competing with other suburban pretenders for the eye of a rich client and the agony of a south Dublin wedding packed with guests I hardly knew and had invited only because they had university degrees – or would act as bouncers if my drunken Aunty Geraldine turned up.

No, I, Kay O'Hare wasn't going to rely on some wrinkly arsed rock legend, surgically preserved film star or pasty-faced computer geek to put a glass roof over my head and a heated swimming pool under my tummy – not in my own birthplace.

Instead, I was planning to be as rich as any of those immigrants; all I needed was a blow-dryer, a few combs and a bleaching kit. I'd keep the beautiful people looking gorgeous – and they'd keep me in Belgowan.

So I left school at sixteen and enrolled in hairdressing academy, where I made lots of OAPs bald, burned the heads off hard-up students and got a few scalp(ing)s under my belt before I was finally given my certificate and told to find a job in a real salon.

'Why do you want to be a hairdresser?' the elegant lady in the black tunic and palazzo trousers asked me during my first job interview at a big Dublin salon. She was the manager and was probably only twenty-five years old, but she looked the height of graceful middle age to me, with her dry orange skin and streaky long blonde hair. In those days, I hadn't yet discovered make-up that could cover my zits, my hair was short, mousy brown and growing out in all directions – and I wasn't yet savvy enough to spot that her suit was a high street knock-off (as opposed to the designer rip-offs I'm used to seeing these days on my social climbing clients – and my VIPs' measured-by-Valentino versions).

'Ever since I was seven, it's been my destiny to be a hairdresser', I told her with a smile I had practised from watching toothpaste ads (though my teeth were crooked and full of fillings, thanks to a diet of fizzy drinks and curry chips). Well, I could hardly tell her my next-door neighbour had forbidden her daughter to play with me because I had chopped off her bunches the day before we made our First Holy Communion. Anyway, Roz was still my best friend and now she had a lovely head of long, red hair, so the pruning must have made it grow stronger.

The woman took me on as an apprentice – in other words, a human toilet duck (the initiation and the cleaning duties), floor-sweeper and remover of hairs from washbasins.

I was the most junior of juniors in that big salon in the centre of Dublin, and I was ready to go places – but the only place I wanted to be was Belgowan. While my mates were talking about flying off at the end of their apprenticeships to work in London, New York, Paris, Milan and Tokyo, I knew I'd find all the glamour I'd ever need in bubbly Belgowan. Well, all those VIPs couldn't be wrong, could they?

I didn't know at the time that Ireland had become a tax haven for anyone who patronised the arts (of politics and creative accountancy); I was exempt from tax because my apprenticeship pay was below the poverty limit but my Dad was paying half his roadsweeping wages in tax so I assumed that rich people would be paying even more.

And I hadn't realised that Belgowan's main attraction was the fact that it was just a helicopter hop from Dublin airport, gateway to the designer showrooms of Europe. The kind of people who had moved into my native town wouldn't be shopping in Dublin's swankiest department stores (lest they'd bump into ambitious groupies and their mothers).

But they would need a local hairdresser to retouch their roots before facing their personal shopper at Harrods or their favourite barman at the Paris Ritz.

So there I was, commuting on a grimy double-decker bus from the wilderness of west Dublin to that big salon in the city every day, perming and straightening my way to a better life, when I met Shay. At seventeen, he was just a few months older than I was, and he had big plans too. 'I'm going to be Ireland's answer to Vidal Sassoon', he told me one morning during our cigarette break in the rain. Even before the Government banned smoking at work, my bosses had banned smoking in the salon; the manager said it was a health hazard (which I suppose it was with all those chemicals in the place).

'When I'm twenty-five', Shay used to say to me; 'I'll be smoking a big fat Cuban cigar, I'll be wearing a Versace shirt and I'll be dying Geri Halliwell's bikini-zone to match her hair.' At least he wasn't gay – and that, in a profession chock-a-block with gender-benders, was dead rebellious. I liked the smoking, too; we shared the same politically incorrect attitudes (well, as anyone with their finger on the fashion pulse would have known, non-PC was soon going to become the new PC).

I fell for Shay big-time. He wasn't anything like Robbie Williams (still my favourite fantasy, no matter how much those ageing pop critics
sneer), but he was all man (well, at least all-adolescent-becoming-man). I can still see us the way we were at seventeen. He had a total bleach-up with matching sideburns and goatee (which my Mam said was 'like the fluff on a badly plucked chicken', but I thought it was very Johnny Deppish especially with his brown eyes), and he was all dressed in black so he looked like Darth Vader's sexier cousin. With his sallow complexion (he grew up beside the gasworks), even his spots were refined.

I had my hair in neon-pink afro-braids, which were cool with my platform combat boots, wide-legged jeans and a 'Fuck me' T-shirt (Shay got the message on our first date, right there in the back row at the matinée of *Star Wars Digitally Remastered*).

That summer, it never stopped raining, so we spent a lot of time in the cinema, fantasising about which famous movie star might come to live in Belgowan and be our favourite client. Not for us the impossible task of satisfying middle-aged ladies who came into hair salons with photos of Meg Ryan and Jennifer Aniston, asking to look 'just like her'. We were going to be working on the heads that went with the famous hairstyles. I dreamed about giving Nicholas Cage dreadlocks. Shay wanted to work on Sharon Stone – though I'm sure he wasn't thinking about her scalp. I wasn't jealous; I knew Shay loved me and would flirt with beautiful actresses only because it would be good for business.

We didn't know where we'd get the money to open a salon – all our wages went on the cinema and taxis home when we missed the last bus. But we had plenty of time.

Our apprenticeship ended abruptly when I had a major row with Vicky, our manager, over some highlights which had gone a bit wrong (well, actually, the woman's hair had broken off and she ended up looking like Bart Simpson).

'Vicky was totally anal about it. It's not as if I'd murdered the woman', I told Shay as we walked the streets of Dublin, dropping our cvs – and a forged reference on our ex-boss's headed notepaper – into every salon. Shay had left in solidarity with me; his loyalty is, I think, the thing I love most about him.

'Some day you'll be the best hairdresser in Ireland; you'll have your own salon in Belgowan where you'll be the boss', he consoled me.

'We'll both be the boss', I said.

One thing was for sure: Kay O'Hare and Shay Duffy weren't cut out for a lifetime of being yelled at by people like Vicky. We had talent and we knew it; the only problem was that we needed to convince other people that we were worth at least the minimum wage.

It took us seven years to get here; seven hard years working for every salon in Dublin and some good but mostly bad employers. The big salons were good for our cvs and the opportunity to learn from Dublin's best stylists – but there was always an ambitious manager who saw us as a threat. 'You needn't worry about us being after your poxy job; it's your customers we'll take', I couldn't resist saying to yet another Vicky type as she fired us. Shay had a theory that the managers in big salons were all clones; he was sure the salons got them from wholesale suppliers, along with the peroxide and perming lotion.

Penny-pinching owner-managed salons, where they paid us 'under the counter', were the best from the financial point of view; the tax we saved went straight into a building society.

It wasn't enough, though. 'At this rate', I grumbled to Shay, 'it'll be twenty years by the time we can afford a down-payment on a chair in a barber's shop. By the time we open a trendy salon in Belgowan, we'll be old fogies.' I looked at the two of us in the mirror. 'Imagine what it will be like when we've gone out of fashion, Shay? Younger people will call me "that nice lady in the combat trousers and belly-top". They'll call you "that old fart with the goatee and the seriously retro post-modern sideburns". You'll be using Grow Fast Anti-Baldness lotion on your head instead of your face. We'll probably be doing special offers for pensioners – instead of blue rinses, they'll be having blue Mohicans to go with their Doc Martens and ripped drainpipe jeans, and the only well-heeled clients we'll get will all be dressed like Crystal Carrington from *Dynasty* and they'll be listening to A-ha on their Walkmans to drown out Radiohead.'

'Jayz', Shay said, letting his cigarette fall from his lips in shock. 'We can't let that happen.'

So I asked my Dad to call the only person who might be able to help us: Councillor Mickey Finn. He didn't remember my Dad at first, which was strange considering the fact that Dad was always sweeping the main street in Belgowan where Councillor Mickey parked his Merc every morning on his way to his local clinic – which was still in the Mad Fiddler.

'They've changed the name of the pub', Dad told me. 'It's called Mental now – I suppose they think that's "way out, man" – and they've changed the decor. The counter is black marble and the chairs are so narrow you wouldn't want to have a bad back. None of the old crowd was there – Jazzer and Brainy have to buy cans in the off-licence and drink at home, because the prices are too high and the atmosphere isn't the same. The place is full of Cormacs and Declans in rugby shirts and skinny birds drinking cocktails. The barmen are all Eye-talians and they can't understand you when you ask for a "pint of the black stuff" – I couldn't even hear myself with that loud pop music.'

Councillor Mickey had changed too, Dad said. 'He's cut off the ponytail and sold the Miami Vice suit to Oxfam. Now he's got gel in his hair – well, what's left of it – and he's wearing a suit by some French designer, or so he tells me. He fits in well with his new constituents, fair play to him.'

After twelve pints of beer, Councillor Mickey pulled a few strings and got the manager of our building society in Belgowan to give us a mortgage on the old Credit Union premises on the main street. 'I'll be buying him beers for the rest of his life for that', Dad told me. 'And you'll be doing his hair and all his family's for free.'

'I'll pay you back, Dad. Don't worry: I'll be the biggest success ever to come out of Belgowan.'

'I know you will, petal. Just don't expect your mother and myself to pay for your wedding – we can't afford it.'

'Oh, that's all right, Dad: Shay and I don't believe in marriage. We're going to live together.'

So, the same cold January week that we opened the salon, we fell out with all four of our deeply Catholic parents and moved into a bedsit over the quaint old post office in Belgowan. The postmistress, Mrs O'Toole, was the same old biddy I remembered from my childhood; obviously the new locals thought she was of historical value. She was old enough to be a listed building, anyway, and just as damp and miserable.

'There's to be no playing of loud pop music at night. This is a respectable area now', she warned us, wagging her finger. She tacked a long list of rules inside the door, which were aimed at turning us into recluses with a cleanliness obsession. I threw the list in the bin. 'Well, she told us to throw away rubbish', I said to Shay.

Our first night in the bedsit was a big adventure for us. It was a Sunday night and we were due to open up the salon for the first time the next morning. To celebrate our independence, we got a Chinese take-away (which we had to eat with our hands because we'd forgotten to ask for plastic forks) and plonked ourselves down on the second-hand flower-patterned sofa we had found at a car-boot sale that morning (there was a smell of farts off it and what we hoped were the hairs off a ginger cat, but it was our first piece of furniture so we thought it was cool). We tried to watch Steven Seagal blow the head off some scumbag on our rented video, but we found ourselves criticising the hairstyles – so we switched off the telly and just talked.

'Shay, do you think the name will put people off?' I still wasn't sure about the name my brother Starsky had chosen while under the influence of Ecstasy.

'Not at all: "Ugly" hits the spot in a place where everyone is tired of being described as "the beautiful so-and-so". A bit of irony will really stand out here. They'll think it's clever.'

Shay always has a calming effect on me; I'm the nervy one. Still even he wasn't totally confident. I knew because he was smoking one fag after the other without finishing them. I was biting my nails and smoking – which is kind of hard to do unless you're really worried.

'Kay', he said to me at last, 'do you remember anything at all from that business course?'

I reflected, blowing smoke up at the yellow cracked ceiling. We had spent every Thursday night for the past two years learning about book-keeping, cash-flow management and filling out tax forms ('But isn't that what bleedin accountants are for?' had been my reaction when I had found out what we'd be learning; I had been delighted to leave maths behind in school but there I was, doing sums all over again). We had kept to ourselves during the coffee-break, partly because none of the other students followed us out to the car park for a smoke, and mostly because they all had middle-class accents and had been sent by their daddies to learn how to run the family tax-evasion business. There were no shopkeepers' sons and daughters; obviously they learned on the job. In the end, we were proud to get our certificates; we were two entrepreneurs with working-class backgrounds (well, Shay's dad wasn't actually working but, as my own dad used to say before he became a road-sweeper: 'Queuing for that unemployment assistance makes a man fierce thirsty.').

'All I can remember', I said to Shay now; 'was the wanker sitting in front of us with the eighties haircut.'

Ugly was going to open in style – we were making sure of that, with a wine and cheese reception. In hindsight, it probably wasn't such a good idea to serve cheap plonk to a clientele that had summer houses with vineyards. But it had been donated free by Anto Byrne, one of Dad's drinking pals out in Ballyskanger. Anto had assured us that the crates had 'fallen off the back of a lorry'. I'd heard that before, so it must have been a common enough occurrence. Anyway, who were we to argue with a man who breeds pitbull terriers and is known as 'Psycho' to the local cops?

Anto was the first person in the door – with one of his pitbulls. 'She needs a good wash. And me missus will be in for a perm tomorrow.'

Our families dropped in too. Our parents hold grudges only when we're the only ones within earshot (they're very friendly in front of everyone else), and anyway they were dead curious to meet each other (they were obviously still hoping we'd have a wedding, which for them is second only to a funeral as an excuse for getting pissed).

'Jaysus, son, you've done us proud', Shay's dad said, as he stared in wonder at the peach-coloured walls, black chrome furniture and black marble washbasins.

We had decorated it ourselves on 'sick days' off from our last job. Our boss had been livid when we had handed in our notice two days before we opened the shop. 'Youse can feck off now – and I'm not payin youse for the last week!' she had yelled. Two weeks had been too long to spend in that place, where the typical client was a tattooed ladies' wrestling champion who wanted a fuzzy perm to go with her shiny leisure suit.

I suppose Shay and I were becoming snobs, much as we tried to pretend we weren't – but snobbery was just a business tool, along with the decor and the cool name over the door.

'Ugly.' We went outside and gazed at it again. 'See, Ma, "ugly" is the new beautiful', Shay said to his mother.

'Well, then your next client will have fellas burstin out of their trousers', Mrs Duffy replied. 'She should have a gun licence for that face.'

The woman she was looking at was wearing an expensive trouser suit, however, and her hair had been cut in a chic blond bob by an excellent stylist about two weeks before. But it did nothing to hide her face.

'My favourite stylist is in Paris', she said in an accent as English as Sterling. 'But you shall have to do.' She stalked past me and sat down on one of our new chairs – you'd think it was filthy, the way she perched on the edge of it. She took a packet of cigarettes and a silver lighter out of her Chanel handbag (I knew it was Chanel because my sister Bernie had bought a fake one on the street). 'I'll have a cappuccino – without the chocolate', she said.

I went into the little kitchen at the back of the salon to see if I could conjure up some cappuccino using an electric kettle, instant coffee and some UHT milk mini-cartons I'd nicked from McDonalds. I rolled my eyes towards Shay. 'Use all the charm you've got', I whispered.

Shay winked at me and swaggered out into the salon. I listened from the kitchen. 'So, what have we got here, Madam? A special occasion – the Oscars, perhaps?'

I cringed, but the lady had the kind of self-confidence that even sarcasm can't penetrate (not that my Shay was deliberately being sarcastic: it's just the Dubliner in him).

When I brought her the mug of instant coffee with lots of UHT milk in it (and some fizzy tonic water to make it frothy), she hardly noticed. She was looking up at Shay in the mirror with a girly smile, and simpering: 'Actually, I am a close friend of Jack Nicholson' (so that's how he practised the expression he needed for *The Shining*, I thought).

'Tomorrow', she was going on, 'I'm flying over to London for a court hearing. I'm suing the arse off my ex-husband. He's Ted Wisebuy – you know, Wisebuy Hypermarkets. They're all over the States. I'm Marina, his second wife. He totally ruined my modelling career. I mean, look at these wrinkles – all his fault.' She pouted as much as anyone can with puckered lips.

She was the only paying customer we got on our first day, so it was just as well that Shay convinced her that she'd look 'only too gorgeous' with red and brown stripes in her hair. 'Go into court looking like that and the judge will give you anything. Baldy old Ted Wisebuy won't stand a chance', he said as she gave him a fifty euro tip.

'Shay', I said when she had gone, 'are you sure she'll come back to us?'

'She will', he said puffing his chest out in the stretchy black shirt he had bought for a fiver in a city centre shop which sells only acrylic clothes. 'With a face like that, the hair wins. She'll get compliments as soon as she turns her back.'

My parents arrived around lunchtime and tried to get us to go to the chipper for lunch. But we had to stay open for business – anyway, Massimo had put up his prices. 'A bleedin fiver for a bag of chips!' Dad grumbled as he and Mam plonked themselves on our black chrome sofa to enjoy their curry chips.

'Jaysus, Kay, have youse no decent magazines?' Mam asked as she flicked through *Vanity Fair*, *Harpers and Queen*, *Image*, *U Know Who* and *IT Girls magazine*.

'I'm going out to get the *Daily Mirror* or *The Star*', Dad said. 'There's no Page Three in this poxy paper.'

'Dad, *Sins on Sunday* has more nude women than all the tabloids put together. That's why most people keep it a week. And more educated people read it, such as politicians and architects and solicitors – you know soliciting used to be the same thing as prostitution, so that's why they like looking at dirty pictures.'

But arty photos of lesbian theatre performers and two-page spreads about saggy old naturists letting it all hang out (they needed two pages to show it all) don't cut it with a man as discerning as my dad.

My parents left after some woman called the cops because Mam's car was blocking the entrance to the woman's auctioneer office. Mam's car was a clapped-out Toyota Starlet, original colour either yellow or red (depending on which door you scrutinised), and now mostly orange (partly from natural causes). My brother Starsky affectionately nicknamed it 'the Zit' and the name stuck, as it would. It hadn't had its annual compulsory safety test for at least five years (the cost of paying a mechanic to test it would have been more than the value of the car), so Mam didn't want the cops anywhere near it.

'Get away from me bleedin car', she screamed as Sergeant Rory O'Reilly used a tissue to wipe away the dust on the licence plate.

Sergeant Rory remembered her. 'What brings you back to these parts?' he asked pompously. 'I'd have thought there'd be plenty of big supermarkets to lift out in Ballyskanger.'

'One thing's for sure', Mam snapped back. 'There'd be nothin worth nickin where you come from.'

Sergeant Rory is from 'the country' which, as all true Dubliners know, is a vast wilderness where obscene quantities of cops are grown on huge farms, covered in fertiliser and left to ferment before being bus-ed to Dublin to torment decent folk.

The woman who had called Sergeant Rory was pacing in front of a big grey Range Roller, a mobile phone in her hand (well, it was either that or she was trying to pick her ear and rub her nose at the same time).

'Hey, missus, will you get off the bleedin phone and move your van?' Mam yelled at her.

The woman turned to look down her nose at Mam (which must have been awful from Mam's point of view). 'I beg your pardon?' she sniffed, wrinkling her nose.

'Your van. It's parked in front of my daughter's hair salon and that's why I had to park in front of that poxy house-vendor place.'

'I haven't got a van', the woman said.

'I've just seen you getting out of it', Mam retorted.

'Oh, the Range Roller.'

Rather than let the conversation take its natural course (Mam has a tongue that would cut steel but that's nothing to her karate chops), I rushed out and handed the woman a complimentary blow-dry voucher, on which we had had printed 'Ugly. We'll sort out your bad hair days. Just drop into Shay and Kay – OK?' She needed it; her hair was perfect for an auctioneer ('Going, going, gone!').

Just to be on the safe side, I gave Sergeant Rory a handful for himself and the other cops. He looked surprised; cops don't usually need vouchers. I thought it

was a discreet way of showing him that he needn't expect freebies. 'Anyway, he'd be a bad ad for us', I said to
Shay. 'You can't do anything with hair that spends its life under a cap and grows out of a bonce shaped like a turnip.'

Keeping in with the cops is only part of running a business, as anyone who's ever had a shop can tell you. Still, we weren't too enthusiastic about Councillor Mickey's idea. 'The Chamber of Commerce. Sure that's full of people who wear big ugly necklaces over their business suits – I've seen them in the local paper.'

'You need to network a bit. They're the kind of contacts you need; they can help you, advise you. Look on it as a kind of insurance – by the way, one of my friends in the Chamber can insure your shop at a very competitive rate.'

'No, thanks, Mickey', I said. 'I'd rather pay Hobbler Byrne, who used to look after all the pubs and shops in Belgowan when I was a kid. Is he still here?'

Councillor Mickey's face turned purple and the whites of his eyes showed. I thought he was getting a heart attack. Then he growled, grinding his teeth: 'Hobbler Byrne has been locked up in Mountjoy for running protection rackets. Don't you dare bring the likes of him around here. Anyway, that kind would burn down your shop if you didn't pay the protection money.'

'Well, what would the Chamber of Commerce do if we didn't pay?'

Councillor Mickey didn't have an answer for that.

Still, Shay and I chatted that night and we decided that joining the Chamber of Commerce might be good for business. 'Look at the heads on those', I said as we pored over the pictures from the Chamber of Commerce dinner in the local paper. 'Seriously in need of a good chop.'

So, the following Saturday morning, we closed the shop and walked two miles in the driving rain along the cliff road to the big hotel where the Chamber of Commerce was having a 'social brunch', as Councillor Mickey had told us. He had promised to give us a lift in his Merc, but since when have politicians kept promises?

'Shay, my feet are killing me', I said as we stumbled, sweating and panting, in through the revolving door and took off our anoraks. I was wearing my platform boots and my new satin-look black trouser suit – I had to keep the jacket closed because I was wearing a belly-top underneath, but it was the only thing that had a modest neckline. Shay was in his best black jeans and a Pucci-print shirt that wasn't by Pucci or even Gucci but looked just as good as anything in the glossy fashion magazines, I thought. He'd gelled his hair into little twisting spikes and was wearing the new aftershave I'd bought him in the One Euro Shop (everyone in Dublin calls it the 'One Euro – or Less' shop because it's such a rip-off and the security staff look like muggers; I thought it would be the right place to buy something for our first day in a protection racket club).

The receptionist looked as if she had piles, the way she was scrunching up her face and rising slowly off her chair. 'May I help you?' she said without moving her mouth (maybe it was to stop the lipstick moving; any farther above her upper lip and it would be in her nostrils).

'No, you're all right, love. We know where to go', I said and we walked arm in arm into the big dining room. I knew my way around the hotel; all my aunties had had their wedding receptions there. This was where we had held Starsky's Coming Out party (coming out of prison, that is; our Starsky's not gay, despite plenty of encouragement from his cellmates).

You could have heard a goldfish fart as we walked into the big room. Rows of men in pinstriped suits and a few women in Mrs Thatcher costumes glared at us. No one looked like they got on well with hairdressers.

'Oh, Shay', I said, clutching his arm, 'where's Councillor Mickey?'

'I don't know, love. It looks as if we're on our own here.'

Councillor Mickey wasn't the most reassuring person, anyway, so I decided we could manage better without him. We weren't going to be intimidated by a few old baldy blokes with fat stripy ties; we were Ireland's finest hairstylists. I whispered to Shay: 'Fuck them all.'

'No thanks', he sniggered.

A waiter in a red shiny waistcoat and greasy black hair came over with a menu in his hand. 'Wayne Faulkner!' I recognised my old neighbour immediately; he hadn't changed since he was nine, except for the height.

'Jayz, it's little Kay O'Hare. How's it going? I heard you got hitched to some tosser –'

'Hey, watch what you say, mate', Shay growled, but he was grinning. It was good to see a friendly face, even if it was covered in zits.

Wayne found us our places and left us. We were sitting opposite each other, which I found a bit cold and unsociable because the table was too wide to whisper across. So I was forced to talk to the man on my right (the one on my left had got up the minute I sat down).

'How'ya. I'm Kay O'Hare. I'm a hairdresser', I said and stuck out my hand.

He kissed it and looked at me with deep brown eyes. 'Ees thees Alcoholics Anonymous?' He nearly blinded me with the glare from his peroxide-white teeth. 'I am Luigi Benvenuto. I have bought a leetle restaurant in thees town: Il Pasticcio. You must come for deener some time. At last I see that ees true what they say: in Dublin the girls are so preetty. These others –' he gestured with a smooth brown hand towards one of the Mrs Thatcher sisters – 'are such a deesappointment'.

'That's because they're all blow-ins. I was born here', I said proudly.

Luigi introduced us to a friend of his, a boutique owner called Charisse. 'Charisse is from California. She used to work on the feelm sets as a wardrobe meestress – and meestress to the stars', he said with a wink.

Charisse was the most glamorous woman I'd ever seen. She had big green eyes ringed with black kohl (they reminded me of my Aunty Geraldine's cat the way it looked when it ate one of Starsky's funny cigarettes) and she was slim without having the horse face that usually goes with diets at her age. The only thing I didn't like about her was her hair, which was red and huge (actually, it looked like a fire in a mattress factory).

When she spoke, it was like listening to someone in a film (I'd never heard a live American accent before except from old American ladies with green trousers who come over to walk in the St Patrick's Day parades). 'Oh, haven't you got just the cutest little Irish face I've ever seen? Those pretty blue eyes and that petal complexion with the little freckles! You must come into me and we'll fix you up with some nice outfits. The others –' she rolled her eyes around the room – 'should be sued by the people who designed the clothes, for giving them a bad image.'

Charisse had used the money from her second divorce to set herself up in business and was planning to clean up in Belgowan – though not among the super-rich. 'Who needs the Hollywood set, honey? It's the middle-class ladies who buy off-the-peg designer outfits: mothers of the bride whose daughters are marrying chartered accountants, débutantes – I think it's so charming you have débutantes in Ireland, even though you haven't got a queen to present them to – and girls who need outfits for Ladies' Day at the Dublin Horse Show.'

She gave us a lift back in her aquamarine green convertible and we promised to drag her hair into the twenty-first century.

Regrowth

It was Macker who showed us just how much Belgowan had changed – for the better, even though he didn't see it that way. It was our second week open and business was still as slow to grow as a bad haircut. We were gawking out the window, hoping that a customer would come in and ask for a complete head of highlights, when we saw Macker getting out of his rusty brown van. He had parked it outside the restaurant across the road, which used to be Mrs O'Toole's hardware shop. Now it was called 'Outré' and it specialised in seafood menus.

'Hiya, Macker!' I yelled and he dropped the crate he was carrying.

'Me feckin foot is broken – Jaysus, it's yourself, isn't it? Little Kay O'Hare?'

He limped across the street and gave me a big, fishy-smelling hug. 'It's great to see you after all these years. I heard you were opening up the salon, and I was meaning to come in to have me beard trimmed.'

Macker's beard is long, red and matted, like the old nets he drags up from the seabed off Belgowan. You'd probably find fishhooks in it if you looked closely enough.

'Ah, your beard is grand, Macker. No one would recognise you if you got it trimmed.'

Macker wrinkled up his forehead and snorted. 'Not recognise me? Sure, I don't even recognise meself these days. Take a look in this box and you'll see what I mean.'

He hobbled back across the street, pulling a penknife out of his jeans pocket, and began prising open the lid of the crate. Shay and I followed him. I expected to find a conger eel as thick as a man's arm wriggling around inside, but instead the box was crawling with lobsters.

'Ugly big creepy crawly things', Macker was growling. 'That's all they want from me now, and it's fierce hard work separating them from the other stuff – I have to keep them alive. The chefs in these restaurants won't buy them any other way. It's their patrons, you see; these fillum stars and prima donnas are paranoid about things not being fresh enough. They won't put anything in their mouths unless it jumps up off the plate and bites them – or pinches the nose off them, as is the case with lobsters. Sure isn't it that why they're always getting new noses? God be with the days when I used to sell the auld grey mullet to Massimo's take-away; all I needed to do was anchor meself near the sewerage outflow pipe. Now the bleedin pipe has been replaced by a fancy thing that goes out half a mile and there's hardly a fish like that to be found. It was that Councillor Mickey who wangled the European Union grant to get a new treatment system put in, and got rid of the old pipe – unhygienic, he says. Unhygienic me arse! This town is going down the bog, with all these nobs movin in.'

Macker spat on the ground and pulled a packet of fags out of his grimy pocket. He grunted, but I said 'No thanks'; Macker's pockets are used for storing bait. He held the packet out to Shay, who looked at me first, then said; 'Thanks, but I'm giving them up.'

Poor Shay was totally out of his depth listening to Macker. 'Isn't a mullet supposed to be blond, like Rod Stewart's?'

'Sure, isn't that what I'm telling youse? These celebrity types are weird. Maybe someone told him it's supposed to be attached to the end of a rod.'

'Which end should it be attached to?' Shay cut in. 'You don't mean – Jayz!'

'Stuck-up arseholes, the lot of them', Macker was going on. 'Swaggerin around the harbour with their fancy anglin equipment. Meself, I only use a net.'

'Annette?' Shay was looking even more bewildered.

Macker grinned. 'So this is the young lad you've shacked up with. Pleased to meet you, son.' He grabbed Shay's hand and shook it the way I've seen him flush the bilge pump in his little trawler.

'I'll tell youse what: I'll give youse a trip on *The Mermaid*. You should see some of the houses they're building on the cliffs here since all that fancy crowd came in. What day have youse off?'

'Tomorrow morning would be good, wouldn't it, Shay?' I looked at him. 'I mean, we haven't got any bookings; we might as well have a break while we still can.'

So the next day we met Macker down at the little harbour. *The Mermaid* was as rusty as ever and her bilge still stank like the back-end of a rat, but as she jogged out of the harbour belching black smoke, I felt I had really returned to Belgowan.

Shay had never been on a boat before, unless you count the 'vomit comet' to Holyhead, where Dubliners go to buy cheap booze. I made him take a whole packet of seasickness tablets before we went out, so he was a bit dopey, but you could see he was enjoying the trip. Macker threw a big anorak at us and we huddled together inside it because there was a nippy breeze, even though it was sunny. It was about as good as you could expect for the middle of winter.

'It's a pity the Hollywood crowd didn't bring some of the weather with them', I said to Macker, who just grunted.

We went down the coast, and I looked up at the cliffs. Some of the houses had little jetties and powerboats parked alongside. Others had slipways from their gardens. Steve Oldman's mansion had its own little harbour. I borrowed Macker's binoculars to see if I could get a peep at Steve, who's the lead singer of Jurassic Rox, but all the curtains were closed; it was only eleven a.m. and sixty-five-year-old rock legends need their beauty sleep.

The cliffs got smaller as we went south; here, I could see the lawns which ran onto the beach. Macker gave a running commentary which was far more interesting than the sort my Aunty Geraldine said they do for tourists on boat trips around Miami; maybe Macker had a new career in front of him, but he didn't know it.

'Do youse see that old Victorian house with the turrets like you'd find on a castle? That's where the rapper Sniffa Dawg lives. He's built a swimming pool in the basement and a recording room in the stables.... That white Spanish villa thing over there is new. It was specially built for the fella who lives there. He used to be the drummer with that old Swedish rock group with the tight jumpsuits – they were around at the time of Gary Glitter, but for the life of me I can't remember their names.

'Do youse see that monstrosity with the pink walls? That used to be a Georgian mansion, and now look at the state of it. It belongs to that Indian singer-actor fella who dances like Michael Jackson and sings like Elvis; he's made it big in Bollywood. It used to be old Brigadier Sir Philip Sherry's house – I never thought I'd say it, but the old British rajahs at least had taste.

'That one with the helicopter in the garden belongs to that serial killer; he's a celebrity now, you know. He wrote a book in prison and when he got out, he was on every talk show in the States. He's making a movie about it. Nice enough guy when you get to know him; he gives a lot of money to charity, stays friends with all his old schoolmates from the trailer park where he grew up. Not a bit snobby.

'And that there's Doctor Chad Wokemann's new clinic for lesbian necrophiliacs.'

'Wha'?' Shay suddenly woke up; I gave him another seasickness tablet and he dozed off on my shoulder again.

'At least that's what that writer fellow told me', Macker said, scratching his beard. 'He lives in that house over there.'

He pointed to a dark wooden house, like the one in 'Psycho' but wider. There were lots of dark graveyard trees around it and a lawn running onto the beach.

'George Morton's his name. He writes those books everyone reads on the toilet – you know the kind you can't put down? Not even when they bring you to the edge of your seat! Me missus is always givin out to me for readin them in the mornin when the kids are goin to work. They're full of spies and cagey characters who swap briefcases loaded with explosives at airports: suave types who wear Armani suits but think nothin of gougin out some diplomat's eyes or shaggin some bird and then stranglin her. He makes a bleedin fortune from writin that stuff. You'd think he'd splash out and pay the barber to give him a decent haircut.'

'Hair?' Shay was wide awake now. 'Did you say he needed his hair done?'

'Too right he does. He came into the pub the other day lookin like the wolfman. Maybe he should be writin horror stories – Jaysus, would you look at the tits on that one!'

He grabbed the binoculars and we had to wait until the boat started drifting, so we could grab them off him while he ran for the wheel. Shay and I banged our heads together trying to look through them; Shay for obvious reasons, myself because I'm just nosey.

We saw a dark-haired, suntanned woman lying on George Morton's beach. She was wearing skimpy black bikini bottoms and nothing else (unless you counted the silicone that she was obviously wearing under her skin; you could tell because, even though she was on her back, her chest looked like two of those blancmange things my granny used to make for Sunday dessert).

'Must be Mrs Morton', Shay said, handing back the binoculars to Macker, who had dropped the anchor.

'Yeah, that'd be herself. I've only met her once, in the pub with Morton. She was wearing more clothes, but I'd recognise that figure in anything. I wonder who the geezer with her is?'

He handed me the binoculars; now it was my turn to give my eyes a treat. No wonder Mrs Morton wasn't feeling the January cold. The guy rubbing suntan lotion into her was the image of Keanu Reeves. He looked far too young for Mrs Morton, who I reckoned was in her forties – but then she was obviously far too glamorous for a man with a wolfman hairstyle.

We spotted him immediately. We had been waiting half an hour in the lounge, trying to ignore the stuck-up college girl who cleaned our table every five minutes, when George Morton shuffled in and sat down in the corner opposite ours. He was alone, and obviously didn't want to be disturbed; I saw him take a spiral notepad and biro out of the pocket of his expensive tan-coloured Crombie, and start scribbling.

'Fortune favours the bold', I said to Shay. 'My teachers always said I was bold.'

I walked over to where George Morton was sitting and sat down opposite him. He looked up. I noticed his forehead was the kind you get when you frown a lot, a big veiny drinker's nose and eyes like a cod's (maybe that's why he had got talking to Macker). I wondered if he saw everything in wide angle. Writers were supposed to look at the world from different angles, weren't they?

He was just staring at me, waiting for me to say something, so I spoke first.

'Aren't you the bloke who wrote *The Tripoli Target* and *The Briefcase Bugger*?'

He smiled; the last time I'd seen teeth like that, they'd been on a mackerel.

'You've read my books?' His voice was one of those plummy voices you hear on those boring BBC 2 documentaries.

'Well, not me, but my brother Starsky. He loves novels about terrorists and bombs.' (Well, that was partly true; Starsky watches lots of videos about that sort of thing when he's high; he thinks they're comedies.)

'Well, tell your brother I'd be happy to autograph my latest novel for him: *Danger in Delhi*. I've just returned from a signing at Bookmaster today.'

I was hoping he'd autograph our chequebook; we hadn't had a client all day.

'Tell you what, Mr Morton – can I call you George?'

'By all means.'

'Well, George, my brother and all his friends are big fans of yours. They think your books are dead cool – much better than all that rubbish about sex and drugs and rapper bands. The only thing is, they think you're a young bloke.'

'Really?' He folded his arms and stared at me, the way my Mam always does when she thinks I'm telling lies.

'Yeah, they think you're thirty-ish and have a gorgeous supermodel wife and a black Porsche Carrera – and a modern hairstyle.'

He was chuckling now, quietly, his hands curled over his mouth, leaning on his elbows.

'Here's my card, George. We're only across the road. That's my partner over there; he might start reading your books too.'

Highlights

My Mam always says luck, like the Number Eight bus, comes in threes. While we were waiting for George Morton to drop in for his total make-over, old Mrs Uberman, who has been living in Belgowan since before my granny was born, came rolling down the hill in her chauffeur-driven Bentley, and demanded a hairstyle that would make her look 'like Marilyn Monroe'.

'Not as she is now, of course', I began but Shay winked and cut me short.

'As she was in her prime, Madam.'

Now you've done it, Shay, I was thinking as I glared at him, but I relaxed when he pointed to Mrs Uberman's Labrador retriever, which was steering her over to a chair.

'We could have told her she looked like Pamela Anderson for all she'd know', I said later, removing her hundred euro tip from Shay's collar.

Next, we got a local girl band called 'Rapid', who all wanted extensions – I recognised one of them as Moira, the girl who used to pull my pigtails when I was in lower infants'. But I don't hold grudges. I gave her the best set of waist-length braids I had and she handed me all her dole money. 'It's worth it', she said as she emptied her wallet. 'I'm going to knock that Sniffa Dawg and his bunch of fat-arsed pansies off *Top of the Pops*. Comin over here with his silly lyrics and his California trailer-park accent....'

I stopped listening when I saw what was pulling up outside the shop. It was long and silver, with smoky windows and the kind of music my Mam listens to throbbing out of it. A stocky skinhead in a tight white T-shirt and black jeans was getting out of the driving seat. He opened the back door of the limo and a pair of scuffed black ankle boots and long, skinny legs in stonewashed denims emerged. It was like watching an insect climb out of a crack in the wall.

'C'mere, Shay, look at this', I said.

'Jayz, it's him – your man from Jurassic Rox: Steve Oldman.'

Moira and her two sidekicks ran to the door, kicking each other's shins to get out first. Then Mam arrived and parked the Zit right behind Steve Oldman's limousine – and then the Rapid girls didn't stand a chance.

'Steve, I luv ya! C'mere to me, gorgeous!' Mam flung her arms around him. She came only up to waist-height, but that was fine for her. Steve Oldman was in shock – though his hair always looked like that. He'd been trying to update his image and had decided that punk was back in as far as the front of his head was concerned, but the back was pure heavy metal, all long and shaggy – and, best of all, full of split ends.

'Get the scissors, Shay', I said.

Steve's burly minders had a tough job persuading Mam to put her knickers back on. For a woman who criticises me and Shay for 'living in sin', Mam can be very liberal when it suits her. Maybe if I was shacked up with a rock star she'd approve. Anyway, she only backed off after Steve had autographed the knickers with her lipstick. Steve was a real gent. He kissed her hand and said; 'It's a pleasure, Madam.' She looked as if she was about to swoon on the pavement, but I had other things on my mind – such as how to get rid of those rappers.

Steve's manager sorted that out (I knew he was the manager because he was the only one in a suit). 'Steve needs total privacy', he said in a *Coronation Street* accent. He whistled at two burly beefcakes, who immediately turned themselves into human roadblocks. Moira and the rest of Rapid had their noses pressed against the glass as Steve Oldman sat down in front of our biggest mirror and the other members of the band sprawled on the couches. The drummer, Flash, was as pale and gangling as I remembered him from the covers of my Mam's old CDs, but close-up you could see that his face was wrinkly and he had obviously had Jurassic Pox as a child. His hair was long, brown and frizzy. The bass guitarist, Eric Stuntmeyer, had a head that looked like that fluffy stuff my Uncle Eddie used when he was fixing boilers (I think it's called 'asbestos'). Great, I thought: three for the chop.

A blonde girl in a mini-skirt took orders for sandwiches from the deli.

'Four freshly squeezed orange juices in tall glasses. Three diet bagels with caviar – no onions', she repeated breathlessly.

'And a packet of Rolos – with the wrappers removed and no caramel filling!' the manager ordered.

The girl looked worried, but scribbled it down on a notepad and skipped out.

Steve Oldman threw his metal-studded leather jacket on the floor and another mini-skirted blonde picked it up, using her manicured fingernails to flick away the hairs off the floor. Shay took it from her and hung it reverently in the cupboard, along with our anoraks.

I stood behind Steve Oldman, scissors poised, and said in my most confident voice: 'You'll need a deep conditioning treatment. But first I'll get rid of those horrible split ends.' I winced the way the top stylists in city centre salons do when they're looking at hair like that; it's the professional thing to do.

Steve went all stiff and gave me that snake-eyed look I've seen him do in some of his videos. It was creepy seeing it coming out of the mirror in the salon. 'Listen, darlin', he said in his *Eastenders* accent, 'my fans come to see me on account of my image – and that includes split ends. So just shut up and perm it!'

He slunk into the chair and pouted.

Flash the drummer was looking sulky too. 'Oh, please God don't let him ask to go blond', I whispered to Shay as we mixed the perming lotion for Steve.

'I'd like highlights all over', he snarled. 'And a perm.'

It was our worst nightmare – what if we became notorious as the hairdressers who made Jurassic Rox bald? I was shaking as I put cotton wool around Steve's hairline to stop the perming lotion going into his eyes; I didn't want to blind him as well (though, come to think of it, it might have helped his career and at least it would be a good excuse for his image).

I left Flash's highlights to Shay; it wasn't so long since that awful episode in my first job, and I didn't want another Bart Simpson on my conscience.

Mam had sneaked in the back door, and never had she been so welcome. 'Mam, c'mere; have you got the St Anthony relic in your handbag?'

'Course I have, love. I carry it everywhere with me.'

'Mam, I know you're still a bit annoyed with me for living in sin with Shay, but I promise you, we'll get married if you pray to St Anthony for Steve Oldman's hair not to break off.'

'Done', she said and gave me a hug.

'And Flash's, and Eric Stuntmeyer's – look, he's getting a perm and highlights too!'

I'm not religious, but St Anthony hadn't been called a saint for nothing, I realised, as Shay and I waved goodbye to three frizzy-haired, permed, high-lighted born-again rockers. They gave us a hundred-euro
tip each – and Steve even winked at my Mam.

After the Jurassic Rox episode, we had more celebrities in our salon than at the Oscars.

The rapper Sniffa Dawg came in with his entourage of girls in belly tops and guys in baggy jeans; they all wanted their heads shaved to within a half-centimetre of their scalps.

Andrew St John, the famous orchestra conductor, popped in to have his grey mop teased out in all directions; he went out looking like a hedge that had been bombed, but that was what the man had asked for.

We always gave the clients exactly what they wanted; the Jurassic Rox perm-up had taught us that. When seventies heart throb Mike Toopay asked for a hairstyle exactly like the one he'd had in *Cool Cops*, we fixed him up with a rug that would shame a Saturday night chat show host (we should know, we did the same 'do' for that TV star all the retirement home babes are raving about – we even glued it on for him).

When Yo Yo Bling, the hip-hop star, handed us half a ton of gold neckchains and asked us to braid them into his dreadlocks, who were we to argue? – even when the weight bent his head back and he was walking out our door looking like something in a horror film (any minute now, I was thinking, his head is going to fall off).

And we knew the difference between small talk and gossip. We needed to, with a clientele that consisted of gossip columnists and their prey. We had to keep secrets because movie stars can't be expected to be discreet; that's for their agents, managers and hairdressers. Famous people love to boast; why else do they choose jobs that involve dancing around stages and gazing into cameras that will beam them onto tellies all over the world? Why else do the less photogenic ones become politicians?

The beautiful, the successful and the scandalous; after a few minutes under our blow-dryer, they were all ready to spill the beans. Long before the tabloid newspapers had got the news, I would know in intimate detail whose husband had run off with a visiting Hollywood actress, and Shay would have enough information to topple the government (whether you were talking about Ireland, Britain or Burkina Faso).

We always stuck conscientiously to the hairdressers' code of conduct, even if it meant staring our favourite gossip columnist in the eyes and telling her that, yes, that actress's luxurious, waist-length hair is all her own and, no, that wasn't the manager of America's top techno band asking us to give them a change of image.

So we weren't reaching for our autograph books when Linda Morton, eighties sex symbol and wife of best-selling writer George Morton, walked in.

I was being hugged by Sniffa Dawg's yoga instructor (who used to be Richard Gere's but got sick of the non-violent end of Buddhism) and didn't see her at first. When I turned around, I saw that Shay had a big grin – and it had nothing to do with the yogi's tip. Linda Morton was elegantly arranged in the VIP chair, flicking back her long black hair and fluttering her sooty eyelashes at Shay.

'It needs a leetle treem, no?'

I remembered having heard that she had been Miss Brazil in the eighties. She had kept the accent – and the figure, which was bursting out of a white silk trouser suit.

While Shay trimmed her hair (and camouflaged the grey regrowth), she told us her life story. She had been born into a rich family who had had some sort of plantation, but the US Marines had invaded it and they had lost their fortune. She had married George when her modelling career was on the way out and her acting career was just getting going.

'See these wrinkles? After my family lost its reputation, those spiteful casting agents on Brazilian TV gave me roles in soap operas, which involved a lot of frowning; now I need Botox injections before I can leave the house. My acting career is destroyed.'

'Why don't you just take more frowning roles and then, when you're really wrinkly, get a massive facelift?'

'Ees not so seemple. When you are older, you will understand.' She patted my cheek, which was a bit spotty that day, and added: 'Or perhaps not.'

When she had gone, I turned to Shay and said: 'I wonder what it feels like to be forty-five years old with a rich husband, two ex-husbands, a French lover who is also a personal trainer, a summer house in Umbria, dinner in Patrick Guilbaud's in Dublin or the Ritz in London, tickets to Andrew Lloyd Webber –'

'Kay, Kay,' he soothed me against his chest. 'Some day, you can have all that if you really want – except the ex-husbands and lover.'

I thought about it for a minute. Then I laughed. 'Nah, it wouldn't suit me. Belgowan and you are all I want – soon we'll be able to afford a little house with a garden for Vidal.'

We had rescued Vidal that morning from a death sentence; the dog warden had found him wandering around the church car park and was about to take him off to be lethally injected when I ran over and snatched him out of the van.

Now he was ours and he was chewing and piddling on every piece of furniture in our bedsit, but we didn't care; we were soon-to-be-rich hairdressers.

'Shay', I said, 'do you think we should get married? I mean, Vidal needs a stable home, doesn't he?'

'Whatever you want, baby', Shay said in his Austin Powers voice, the one he always uses when he's doing something that makes him feel all manly and confident.

'I wouldn't swap you for anyone', I said into his chest. 'Not even Mrs Morton's personal trainer, Pierre.'

'I wouldn't swop you for Mrs Morton', Shay sniggered. 'You know, I met Pierre the other day in the pub; he says she has a lumpy bum.'

Tints

I had loved Belgowan, but I loved the New Belgowan even more. The old hierarchy of snobs ('tuppence ha'penny looking down on tuppence' as my granny used to call them) were being elbowed out by a new elite who didn't know – or care – that Mrs Anchorbottom was Dublin's top socialite or that Mrs O'Hagan's daughter had a good job in the European Commission, or that Councillor Mickey was Ireland's answer to politics – didn't even know that Belgowan was supposed to be an exclusive area.

'Justice at last', I said to Shay. 'These celebrities are just like us.'

We often bumped into Steve Oldman and the rest of the Jurassic Rox crew in the chipper. They were working-class blokes and they loved nothing more than a big bag of greasy fish'n'chips with salt and vinegar. Their yogi disapproved, but one Friday night we caught him sneaking into the Indian take-away for a genetically modified soya satay.

The only famous person I didn't like was George Morton. There was just something, well, creepy about him. Maybe it was those fishy eyes which seemed to have no definite colour and never focussed on you even when he was staring. Perhaps it was the hands – they were as white as a fish's belly but too coarse for a man who made his living tapping a computer keyboard. Or it could have been the way he always came into the salon silently; he was just there when you turned round.

Still, he was our most regular customer, and we couldn't afford to turn him away, as Shay reminded me, so I just ignored the burning feeling in my stomach whenever I saw his name in the appointments book. Once he had seen how good he could look with the right haircut and beard-trim, he came in every week. We had tamed the hair and dyed it a subtle charcoal shade and now he looked like the kind of man who just might have a former beauty queen for a wife – if he happened to be rich enough.

'Now people won't shy away from you on the street because they're afraid you're going to ask them for money', I said to him one morning.

'Maybe I should have kept the old image', he replied. Ungrateful old fart.

He had spent the whole half-hour complaining about a TV adaptation of one of his novels, which was about an ambassador who worked as a spy for a drug lord. 'It's not so much the fact that they changed the plot, the characters, the themes and everything else. What really bothers me is that they gave it the same name as my novel. They could just as easily have called it *Spies in Space* – or perhaps *Snow White*.'

He went on to talk about his passion for shooting birds. The only game I approved of was that street-fighting thing Shay liked to play with his Playstation on our portable TV – so I was shocked when George Morton described the way he had massacred a whole flock of pheasants on the hill that morning.

'A group of pheasants is called a "bouquet",' he corrected me.

No wonder his wife preferred other men if that was what he called a bunch of flowers, I thought; Linda didn't seem like the kind of woman who would enjoy stuffing pheasants into a vase. I supposed that was what the Mortons' chef, Marco, had meant when he'd said George had fired him for 'stuffing his bird' (and probably the reason George had cooked Marco's goose).

I felt like crying, so I told George I'd get him a coffee.

'I don't want one', he said, but I ignored him – and ran into the kitchen before I could make a total plonker of myself in front of the other clients.

Shay came in after me and pulled me against his T-shirt. 'What's up, Kay?'

'That big fat murderer; he kills poor little birds that never did any harm to anyone. He pretends he's going to give them some bagels from that new Greek deli – and then he blasts them away with a semi-automatic pistol that he got off some spook he interviewed when he was researching one of his books. He takes their little lives away and then he hangs their bodies up to rot in his garage and then...then he eats them.'

I couldn't help myself; I covered Shay's fake-Armani T-shirt with mascara.

'I knew by his face'. I was getting angry now. 'He's got these greedy, bulging eyes that stranglers always have in the films of his books. I bet he's not making those stories up at all. A man who's capable of bumping off innocent animals wouldn't flinch at killing international terrorists. And he's got lips like Hannibal Lector's.'

'I know, I know; we'll have to get used to those because Anthony Hopkins is buying a house here. C'mon, Kay, you kept your eyes open through two horror videos last night. Just scalp him and take his money and try not to think about him.'

'Shay', I was brainstorming ahead of myself now. 'D'you know who owns the land that hill is on – the hill with the pheasants?'

'Yeah: Eric Stuntmeyer, the bass guitarist from Jurassic Rox – you look a bit like him with your mascara running down your cheeks, love.' He wiped my face with a tissue. 'So what are you saying?'

'Well, isn't his wife an animal lover?'

Shay sniggered so I added: 'I mean, she loves animals – oh, you know what I mean. Remember that protest she had on the Milan catwalks about fur coats?'

'I sure do! She was the only one who kept up her promise to go naked rather than wear fur.'

I pulled out the diary; Giada Stuntmeyer was pencilled in for highlights the next day. I gave Shay a V sign and inverted it behind the cup of coffee I was bringing out to George Morton. I had laced it with sugar because he had told me he was diabetic. If he drank it, maybe his wife wouldn't need to shag that flashy divorce lawyer she'd flown in from L.A. to get him to waive his fees until she had the settlement; she could afford to fly her impoverished parents over from Sao Paolo; she might even splash out and buy a top for her bikini.

George Morton's voice was smothering the Red Hot Chili Peppers (not the real ones, unfortunately; just their CD, but we were still hopeful). I wished he'd shut up about his sickening 'sports', but he was obviously one of those people who go to hairdressers instead of psychiatrists or the priest.

'There's Father Nick; he'd love to hear your confession', I said. The parish priest was actually coming into the salon.

'That's your Ma's fault', Shay whispered. 'He's probably going to make us do a marriage preparation course and we'll be spending every Monday night in the church hall listening to schoolteacher couples talk about their sex lives.'

But Father Nick had changed. He used to have hair like a donkey's (the parishioners had even nicknamed him 'Father Ned' because he was the spitting image of Father Ted off the telly), but lately he'd discovered hair gel, sunbeds and blue contact lenses, and regularly flew to Rome to buy made-to-measure priest outfits (his favourite had a cloak with a red silk lining and, together with the tan, made him look like George Hamilton in *Love at First Bite*).

Still, I'd heard he had started calling St Edward's 'St Ned's' ever since the film *Waking Ned* had won that prize at the Cannes Film Festival (it hadn't actually been made in Ireland but there was a rumour going around that the star, David Kelly, was moving into Belgowan and now every old geezer with a strong Dublin accent was being helped across the road by leggy lovelies).

With so many movie stars in the congregation, Father Nick really believed in the Hollywood spirit. Mass was now an Oscar-winning performance, he was probably the first priest in Ireland to introduce macrobiotic Holy Communion bread, and the Communion wine was now specially imported from Bordeaux.

He used to hate weddings (whether out of envy or boredom, we never could be sure) but now he was hugging the two of us (and digging his manicured fingernails into our necks). 'It'll be wonderful to have you kids getting married in Belgowan', he was drawling in his new mid-Atlantic accent. 'Our immigrant community is just going to love a quaint Irish wedding with typical local characters.... Oh, by the way, our marriage preparation panel has a guest counsellor: Doctor Erika Slutzberger – you know, the famous sexologist who has her own show on Fox TV and has written, like, zillions of self-help books –'

'My Ma told me self-help sex would make me blind', Shay cut in.

But Father Nick's new theology stretched to the all-inclusive end of liberalism. 'You know Nit and Tick from that, like, totally cool California band Asparagus?'

Yeah, we knew them: Nit had upside-down crucifixes tattooed all over his body and Tick was the bloke who reputedly sucked the blood from young male virgins at concerts.

'Well, they're going to be my first gay couple; they're getting married at St Ned's on Saturday', Father Nick said proudly.

'Oh, by the way', Father Nick added; 'I'll need my hair done, OK? You can both have back-row seats in the Gods – I've no need for that dreary old choir and organist now that we've got real *artistes* playing.'

He sat down in front of the big mirror where all our ultra-VIPs sit and smiled over at George Morton, who was looking moody in his corner seat now that no one was listening to him.

'Hi, I believe I know Linda; great friend of the church. I'm Father Nick Cox – but everyone here just calls me Nick.' (I was tempted to say 'No they don't', but I didn't because New Father Nick would probably sue me for blasphemy if I told him what the natives of Belgowan were calling him these days.) He held out his hand to George Morton, who just frowned and folded his arms.

Father Nick shrugged his eyebrows (which he had darkened to look like George Clooney's) and hummed to himself (it sounded like one of the Asparagus songs from their new CD which had a 'Parental Advisory: Explicit Lyrics' label on the cover).

Then I saw him smile (showing more crystals than the Fworrovski cross Linda Morton had donated for the altar). Barbara Burrows was coming in with a big satisfied smile on her face. She's that lady who writes a (very) social column for *Sins on Sunday*.

'Barbara, what a lovely surprise', Father Nick said, jumping up to give her his seat. She tweaked his cheeks (leaving talon marks in them) and sat down, crossing her legs.

George Morton suddenly got up and walked out, without a word to anyone – and didn't even leave his usual miserly tip. I ran out after him, but he was already climbing into his big green car. 'Let him go', Shay said. 'He'll be back as soon as he realises we only trimmed one side of his head.'

Father Nick and Barbara Burrows were yackering away in their chairs, which they had pulled close together. 'Nick, darling, you have no idea what it would mean to the Duchess of Straththigh to be baptised in St Ned's. She was converted to Catholicism when she saw the picture of you in my column – and she's moving into that converted Methodist church on the hill with her new boyfriend, who is a wonderful up-and-coming movie director.'

As I permed and dyed his hair to make him look like some Italian TV reporter he'd met in the Vatican, Father Nick filled Barbara in on the goings-on at St Ned's. 'We've upgraded the parish resource centre. No more bingo sessions for old dears in surgical stockings and incontinence knickers – eugghh! No more spotty geeks with guitars singing Bob Dylan songs out of tune; no more lay-nuns with no make-up. Now we've got the Miami Gospel Choir holding rehearsals – the ticket sales have paid for a new roof.... Sheikh Ahmed's ex-wives are teaching belly dancing every Tuesday – and I'm not talking about flabby middle-aged ladies doing the Dance of the Seven Veils in customised Wonderbras. The classes are open only to people who've done a tummy-flattening course with your man Pat Henry – you know that seriously cool fitness guru who trains all the celebs when they're in Dublin?

'And you know Sniffa Dawg's yogi, Rasheed? Well, he moonlights as a meditation teacher – actually, I'm having a bit of trouble scheduling all these yogis and gurus and personal trainers who want to run classes there.

'Oh, and we've got Doctor Rowena Edge – you know, the author of those books about empowering women? She's running counselling sessions for postmodern feminists who haven't come to terms with the new "girly feminism". She used to be a nun, you know, but she got defrocked for lesbianism in the bad old nineteen eighties.'

Astrologists, tarot card readers, New Age healers and even Jehovah's Witnesses were also running courses in the church hall; the only thing they seemed to have in common was the fact that they were all either famous themselves or 'famous by procuracy', as Father Nick called it.

He added that the controversial Italian film director Enrico Bendini was going to be giving a guest sermon, followed by a screening in the church hall of the uncut version of his new epic, *Blasfemio Infernale*, which apparently suggests that God is an Italian film director. Even death metal rockers The Chainsaw Crucifixes were planning to hold their own Mass there.

'They told me it would be a "black mass", so I said OK, cool, go with the flow – I'm totally anti-racism.'

Our home-grown rappers, Rapid, had obviously pooled their dole money to give Father Nick a backhander, because he was really putting pressure on Barbara Burrows to mention their concert, which was being held in the church hall to raise funds for a new roof. She didn't seem so keen. 'What's their new song called?' she sighed, doodling on her notepad but not actually writing.

'It's a bit provocative – you know how these rappers have to keep up the hard image? It's called *Jesus Ain't in Da House*. They're working through a lot of anger in it – one of the most memorable lines is: "Momma doesn't deserve my love 'cos she made me go to Mass".'

'That sounds like something Sorcha O'Sullivan would sing', Barbara said. 'You know, she's moving back to this part of the country – she's a fully trained Celtic priestess now, you know.'

Father Nick suddenly looked uncomfortable. 'That Celtic stuff is all a load of old rubbish', he said.

'And the Reverend Vernon Good is coming here to live', Barbara was going on. 'You know, the guy who preaches on American TV?'

Father Nick's jaw was tightening, as if he was getting an invisible facelift. It must have been that expensive moisturiser I had seen him buying in the chemist's a few days before. It's supposed to tighten your skin deep down. Maybe it was working on his voice too; he sounded as if he was being strangled. 'Vernon Good', he was saying. 'Isn't that the guy with the big wig?'

Shay winked at me. 'Now we're talking business', he whispered. 'Shhh!' I replied; hairdressers are allowed to be confessors but not eavesdroppers.

Itchy scalp

I was probably the only native girl in Belgowan whose wedding list didn't include a bridegroom made in Hollywood, but I was happy: I had found what some of those celebrities were still looking for after three divorces, and what some people never even dreamed of finding.

Take my old neighbour, Mrs Murphy. She came into the salon one day, asking for all-over blonde highlights and a cut. 'Not a granny cut, mind you', she cackled. 'I'm going to find myself a toyboy.'

She was just killing time in the salon, asking us to 'give it a good long wash and plenty of conditioner' and hanging around after we'd finished. She wanted to keep out of the house, she explained, because her husband had recently retired from his job in the civil service and was boring her to death.

He had cancelled his membership of the Active Retirement group because (he had claimed in a letter to the local paper) it was full of 'semi-fossilised rock relics sitting around planning their comeback, practising the electric guitar and threatening to replace the Granny of the Year pageant with a Most Glamorous Grammy contest.'

'Now', Mrs Murphy sighed, 'he sits in front of the telly from morning to night, watching the news and complaining about politicians. I can't bring my friends in for a chat because he just turns the telly louder. He's supposed to be fixing the lawnmower, but he's simply taken it apart and dumped it in the kitchen.'

She looked at Shay and pursed her lips, then squinted at me: 'Don't let him wear you out, lovie', she said to me. 'Being stuck with your fella twenty-four hours a day is enough to drive you to drink.'

Mrs Murphy never needed an excuse for drinking, I thought, but I wasn't about to remind her (she'd take back her tip, which was half the price of a pint). Instead, I pushed her gently out of the salon. 'Send Mr Murphy in for a cut', I said. 'It might liven him up.'

Once word got around among my old neighbours that Shay and I were getting married, all the old biddies were ogling my tummy, puckering their lips and nodding at one another, and little Aisling O'Connor even gave me the thumbs up. But that bump was just chocolate and take-away pizza.

I ignored my sister Bernie's warnings about my 'biological time-bomb' exploding; I was still only twenty-three. Besides, one of Belgowan's newest residents was Doctor McClone, the Harley Street 'fertility god', as *Sins on Sunday* called him. Anyway, our Bernie wasn't much of an expert on biology – she'd managed to get pregnant despite taking every precaution. I loved little Robbie as much as she did, but Vidal was enough child for Shay and me.

'Hasn't he lovely scruffy fur?' I said to Shay one day as we were washing him in the salon after hours. 'I mean, no matter what you do with it, it always comes out looking like that stuff you find in the hoover bag.'

We had bleached, permed and dyed Vidal every colour we could think of. He was our very own test-model – and he wasn't complaining. He wagged his long, fluffy green tail and licked one of the plastic containers in the sink. 'Careful, Vidal, that's hydrogen peroxide', Shay laughed.

Just then, Vidal stiffened and whimpered.

'Oh, Shay, I hope he's OK', I said.

But Vidal hadn't been poisoned (he obviously had a hardened street-mutt's stomach). He was looking at the door. Someone was peering in, his big fat nose pressed against the glass.

'It's George Morton. I suppose we can't turn him away', Shay said.

The writer was smiling for a change (it wasn't a pretty sight) and he even said 'Thank you, my dear', when I pulled out his seat. He sat down slowly and crossed an ankle over his knee. He had obviously bought new shoes and was showing them off, so I said: 'I like the shoes, George.' He smiled to himself, then looked around in surprise as Vidal began whimpering in Shay's arms.

'Oh, what a charming little dog! What's his name?'

'Vidal', Shay said, holding Vidal closer. Vidal licked Shay's face and whimpered again.

George Morton was looking surprised now. 'Ah', he said: 'After Gore Vidal.'

'Who's he?' I asked. 'We called him after Vidal Sassoon – the greatest hairdresser who ever lived.'

My Aunty Geraldine says animals have psychic powers. She should know: she's been a professional fortune-teller ever since she was a child, when the tarot cards told her it was her destiny to shuffle them for anyone who paid her a fiver (except now it's gone up to fifty euro). 'It's a pity she can't tell us who's going to win the four-thirty at Leopardstown or the Ireland versus Bulgaria match', Dad says, but he's never liked Aunty Geraldine or anyone else on Mam's side of the family.

Anyway, she was right about animals: they know things the rest of us can only guess at. I felt George Morton was creepy, but Vidal *knew* it, and now he was trying to tell us. He stopped shaking only when George left.

Our landlady, Mrs O'Toole, obviously had ambitions to become Wacko Vacco's cleaning lady (if the rumour was true that the hermetically sealed pop prince was building a germ-free fortress on the hill). She was always disinfecting the stairs and landing outside our door.

She usually did it early in the morning when we were having a lie-in (we never opened the salon before eleven because most of our clients were either jogging with their personal trainers or nursing cocaine hangovers). So we lay in bed, me, Shay and Vidal, trying not to hear the mop thumping against the door.

Sometimes she had a friend with her, and the pair of them bitched about us, as if they knew we were listening. 'Lazy, that's what they are. They wouldn't even clean the landing outside their own door. Sleeping until this hour of the morning!'

'I wouldn't say they're sleeping', Mrs Finnerty would cackle.

'Dirty creatures', Mrs O'Toole would reply and she'd wallop the mop against the door.

We usually waited until they had gone – which often took a few hours – before running downstairs to collect our post. It always looked as if it had been opened. Even the bank envelopes had been stuck with tape. We didn't tell the bank about it – because our account was in the red, so we were trying to avoid the manager. Luckily he was bald (and anyway bank managers make lousy clients: they never leave tips).

One morning, we opened our door and found Mrs O'Toole on her knees with her ear at key-hole level. She leapt to her feet (which was amazing, given that she was always complaining about her bad back).

'Oh, merciful hour!' she screeched. 'Youse nearly gave me a heart attack.'

'Hello, Mrs O'Toole', Shay said; he's always polite to old women because he thinks they cast curses (his granny has more curses than an Egyptian mummy – and Mrs O'Toole is probably as ancient as an Egyptian granny).

'Youse ought to be ashamed of yourselves, leaving your flat so dirty and untidy', she huffed.

'We look after our flat – I mean bedsit – very well', I said, wondering how she knew; maybe she was psychic like Aunty Geraldine, I thought.

'Let me in so I can assess the damage to my property', Mrs O'Toole said, barging past us into our home.

'Is that a dog?' Vidal was sniffing around her fat ankles.

'What does it look like?' I started, but Shay shusshed me.

'He's very quiet, and we've housetrained him', Shay said.

Vidal chose that moment to cock a hind leg and spray Mrs O'Toole's tan-coloured tights.

She gave us a month to get out. 'That'll allow me time to find another tenant', she sniffed.

Meanwhile, we were counting on the chance that she wouldn't cash the cheque for our previous week's rent until we had spoken to the bank manager. Our income was rising but it still wasn't covering our overheads. We were learning the hard way why ex-locals called the town Dear Old Belgowan. The price of beer had skyrocketed, as you would expect in place full of stars, and a Chinese takeaway now cost more than the airfare to Shanghai. We hoped none of our clients would guess that we were using washing-up liquid instead of shampoo.

'Shay, what are we going to do? We'll never find a bedsit as cheap as Mrs O'Toole's – have you seen the rents they're charging in this area?' The area had become so upmarket that even a house-share was expensive – and anyway we didn't want to share a bathroom and kitchen with 'non-smoking professionals' who couldn't afford a mortgage.

'We'll just have to sleep in the salon until we find something', Shay said. 'It's a pity our sofas are all chrome.'

We thought about asking one of our clients to rent us a room, but decided it wouldn't look professional. And the prospect of moving into Aunty Geraldine's two-bedroomed house wasn't very appealing; she surely wouldn't let us watch TV during a séance, and anyway Vidal wouldn't get on well with her cats.

We didn't fancy moving into any of my old neighbours' houses either; nowadays they were all members of the Belgowan Residents' Association ('Nosey Neighbours Incorporated', as Shay called them) and we were sure they'd bully us into sitting through weekly meetings about cracked footpaths and hedges that needed trimming (their coarse greying hair needed an even bigger trimming, but these were the home-styling diehards who still used 'the roundy brush' to create sausage curls).

'Shay, it says here in the *Residents' Association Newsletter* that Steve Oldman attended the AGM.' There was a photocopied picture of his *Greatest Hits* album cover on the front page; just a head-and-shoulders, so he didn't even look like a rocker, just a wrinkly with long permed hair. Inside was a report on the AGM itself; Steve had apparently gone respectable in his old age because the only question he asked at the meeting was something about planning permission for a tennis court at the back of his mansion.

There was an interesting letter from a Mr Feeney, who was going up for election to the local council; he wanted the residents to 'cast aside their prejudices' and agree to his proposal for a travellers' campsite in Belgowan. 'After all, we've welcomed people from as far away as California', he wrote, adding that his plan had the support of many of the town's Hollywood stars.

'This Mr Feeney will give Mickey Finn a bit of competition', I said to Shay. We looked at the badly reproduced black-and-white photo.

'He'd look OK with a good cut', Shay said, sharpening his scissors.

Mr Feeney – Jason, as he wanted us to call him – came into the salon one afternoon, asking for 'something that would look good on an election poster.'

He was younger than he had looked in the *Residents' Association Newsletter*; he was just twenty-nine and had recently 'been called to the bar', as he put it in a Dublin accent as strong as my Shay's. I thought he meant the barman across the road in Mental was looking for him, but he explained that it meant he was a barrister.

'Oh, you mean the lawyers with the wigs? Cool!' Shay said. 'Give us a look at your lid.'

Jason chuckled and pulled it out of his briefcase. It was, as you'd expect, grey with tight little curls. 'It needs a good wash', Jason admitted. 'Normally these things are handed down from father to son, but I'm the first barrister in my family. I found it in the small ads in the *Legal Eagle*. I bought it from the widow of some bloke who passed away about twenty years ago. He must have had some manky scalp disease.'

'Here, give it to us and we'll sort it out', Shay said. 'It'll be no worse than that job we did this morning for the undertakers. Old Mr O'Brien never looked so good when he was alive'. I was getting worried; Shay had that look on his face that he had whenever he was feeling 'creative'. But I was finding it hard to watch Shay, with Jason making eye contact in the mirror. Mickey Finn had already lost the election, as far as I could see.

'There y'are', Shay said after half an hour. Jason was having yet another deep conditioner massaged into his perfectly shaped head and I had to rub the suds out of his eyes to let him see the wig, which Shay was twirling on his fingertips. It was blond. Platinum blond, with gold highlights. And the curls had been loosened a bit.

'Now it's not so, like, *rigid*. You'll start a new trend with this', Shay said. 'It's seriously cool. You'll be the David Beckham of barristers.'

'Massive!' Jason said with a big grin. 'I'm not ready to go grey just yet.' He ran his hands through the suds in his own hair, which was naturally luxurious and, thanks to my magic scissors, now made him look like Colin Farrell. It really was a shame he had to cover it up with a wig at work. 'I'm sure that law about wigs in court was made by baldies with funny-shaped heads', I told him.

He was stuffing the wig into his briefcase when Barbara Burrows walked in. She gaped and clutched my arm. 'Is that – don't tell me it's Colin Farr –'

'Shhh! He doesn't want anyone to know he's here.'

She put a manicured nail to the side of her nose and grinned at me. 'I won't say a word.' Until Sunday, she meant; I could see the headline already.

'There's no point in interviewing him, anyway', I added. 'He's psyching himself up for a part so he's in character.'

Barbara sat down on the chair next to his and leaned forward (she always did this to men when she was wearing a low-cut blouse, I noticed). 'Mind if I borrow a cigarette?' she said huskily.

Jason grinned and gave her the one he was smoking. She nearly fell off her chair. He winked at me and got up, slinging his jacket over his shoulder. He stuffed a wad of notes in Shay's back pocket. 'Buy yourselves a few e-tabs' he joked.

The local elections were temporarily elbowed off the front page of the *Belgowan Residents' Association Newsletter* – by a beauty contest. This was nothing to do with the festival queen pageant which was held every July; there would be no wholesome, toothsome blonde girl-next-door types in puffy home-made dresses riding down the main street on a truck decked out with roses and answering cringe-making questions from Father Nick about their pets and their long-term ambitions to join the foreign missions. This was freezing February, so the selection was taking place indoors – in a suite at the Ardnarock Hotel overlooking the harbour (it had recently been upgraded to four stars but the manager insisted there were more).

It needed to be indoors because the entrants were expected to strip off to g-strings in front of a panel of judges from the upmarket men's magazine, *Bloke*. One of those panellists was sitting in our VIP chair, the day before the contest.

With his pockmarked face and shoulder-length, wispy greying hair, I couldn't imagine famous models blowing kisses at Neil Titwick the way they did in the photo he had taken for that month's cover of *Bloke*. 'The kiss was aimed at the camera, not me', he said, as if he was reading my thoughts.

He had been auditioning girls all week and was looking tired. 'It's 'ard work', he said. 'Especially when there's so little to choose from.'

Well, I wasn't going to let a wrinkly old sleaze-bag from London slag off the local girls, was I? 'Steve Oldman of Jurassic Rox told me he moved here especially for the girls', I said. 'And Miss World came from just down the road.'

'Oh, I didn't mean there weren't any beautiful birds around 'ere. It's just that, most of the time, the really gorgeous ones don't seem to know it, and the rest of 'em 'ave got too much confidence.'

'That's because, in Ireland, we don't believe in giving people swelled heads. And we give ugly people compliments to cheer them up.'

'Oh, I see.' He gave me a sparkling smile (well, what else could he do with crystal studs in his teeth?). 'Cool name for the shop, by the way, "Ugly"; I like it.'

He said he was leasing an apartment in Belgowan for a few months, because he was hoping to travel around Ireland 'in search of untapped flesh'.

'That'll be easy', I said. 'There's no shortage of unspoilt beauties in Ireland – because the men prefer beer.'

He sniggered. 'Oh, by the way, you wouldn't happen to know where Linda Morton lives, by any chance?'

'You know her?' I hadn't seen Linda for a few weeks.

'Yeah. Linda and I go back a long way. We did some great spreads together when I was working for *Playboy*.'

'Shay, have you seen Linda lately?'

'Not a sign of her, love. George came in for a trim this morning and didn't say a word. They've obviously fallen out. Maybe it's over Luigi Benvenuto; one of his waiters caught them making out after hours.'

'Luigi has been living dangerously lately', I said. He was engaged in a feud with Massimo the chipper, who was making it clear that Belgowan was too small for two Italian diners. Massimo had left a battered cod in Luigi's letterbox; Luigi had retaliated with a packet of smoked salmon.

'I don't think Luigi is going to be scared off by a jealous husband', Shay was saying. 'Anyway, George should be used to Linda's social life by now.'

'Poor Linda', I said to Neil Titwick. 'After having such a glamorous life, now she's buried alive with a husband whose hobby is shooting birds.'

'What – 'e's taken up photography?'

Eviction was getting closer and we still hadn't found a new pad. We were thinking about asking the Travellers to rent us a caravan – we could join their lively roadside community until Jason won the election and got them a campsite on the hill above Belgowan (we were sure he'd get elected, with that haircut we'd given him).

'The sooner we find a place, the better. I'd move out tomorrow and let her keep her poxy rent', I said to Shay. 'The bedsit just doesn't feel like our home any more.'

'Funny you should say that. I was just thinkin the same thing. It's too, well, tidy or something.'

'Hey, that's what it is. Shay, have we ever turned our socks inside out and put them in neat little piles in the drawer?'

We went through all our drawers and the wardrobe – somebody else had done so, by the looks of it. Even our bathroom cabinet had been tidied – and the condoms were missing.

'No wonder Mrs O'Toole is anxious to evict us', I said. 'She's a member of Neighbours Against Gays (NAG), which has broadened its scope to include anyone who uses condoms.'

'That's that pressure group that Councillor Mickey and Father Nick are terrified of, isn't it? The one that wants to run all these celebrities out of town because most of them are gay and the rest are sympathisers? Jayz, that's queer – and not very community-spirited. *Neighbours* the fuck! That show has gone downhill since the days of Kylie Minogue and Jason Donovan.'

'I don't think it's anything to do with the soap, Shay –'

'Wouldn't you think those Australian soap stars would be more tolerant of unconventional people, seeing as how they live upside-down? Are you sure you're not thinkin about the cast of *Friends*? I heard there was a campaign called FAG.'

'No, Shay, that's a smokers' rights group. Anyway, Mrs O'Toole wouldn't get involved with soaps – she thinks they're dirty. NAG is just a hardcore bunch of old battleaxes.'

They were threatening to hold a candlelit vigil outside the church on the night before the election.

'Imagine what it will be like', I said to Shay. 'Enrico Bendini's film is going to be screened the same night – it's got some gay scenes.'

'He'll be delighted. He'll get the publicity and some material for a new film – kind of like the KKK in skirts, in modern Ireland.'

'Shay.' I was suddenly walloped in the head with the sort of idea that wouldn't go away until I had done what it told me – the kind that had been getting me into trouble ever since I was in school. 'Shay, I think we need some security cameras.'

'What? For the salon? Ah, Kay, who'd rob us here in Belgowan?'

'I'm not thinking about the shop. We could buy the camera for the shop and get it off our tax – but use it here in the bedsit.'

'Maybe we should just leave Vidal here when we're out', Shay said. But I was pretending not to hear him.

A few days later, we played the security tape in our video and there, in dingy blue-and-white, was a close-up of Mrs O'Toole rummaging through our belongings. We had positioned the little camera on top of the chest of drawers, inside a vase full of plastic flowers that Shay's Ma had bought us as a house-warming present; at last we'd found a good use for them. The camera was a cheap one with a fish-eye lens that made Mrs O'Toole's face swell every time she came close, like in a goldfish bowl. We could see every crevice around her thin lips, which were moving as if she was muttering to herself while she examined my pink glittery g-string, stretching it.

'The old witch', I said. 'She'll make it too big!'

'Jayz, let's hope she doesn't try it on', Shay said. But Mrs O'Toole just folded it and put it back.

'Do you think we should go to the cops about her, Shay?'

'Nah. Sergeant Rory would never listen to us. Let her have her kicks. She's got nothing else in her life.'

'Enrico Bendini, then? Wouldn't it be fun to give him a filmette that he could use in one of those arty black-and-white films he makes? An old woman snooping through a young couple's underwear drawer – that's the kind of thing he has in his films.'

'Kay, can you imagine Mrs O'Toole at the Cannes Film Festival? Anyway, she could sue us for that!'

'She never looks at the films she condemns: she's afraid they'll corrupt her.'

Local election fever was like an outbreak of lice among the town's politicians and their challengers; they were all scratching their heads and demanding a haircut. Ambitions had risen since the old days when the voters were impressed by any candidate who looked half-decent on the billboards. Now they all wanted to be photogenic, and we were happy to oblige as long as they paid.

Councillor Mickey Finn was in with us every morning for a wash and blow-dry. 'I want my hair to look respectable – I need to come across as a normal guy, right? A family man.'

'You are a family man, Mickey', I pointed out. Well, he had children and a wife – and a girlfriend who doubled up as a stamp-licker. What more could a local politician ask for?

'It's the *image* I'm talking about. Make my hair look like the average guy's – you know, the guy who drives a medium-sized BMW, has a normal five-bedroom house, works as a company director, that kind of thing.'

'Jayz, Mickey, when you said "normal" I thought you meant like the blokes you used to call normal – remember when you used to say: "I'm fighting for the normal guy, the man on the street, in his van, saving up his dole money to pay the Council rent"? You used to have it on all your election pamphlets – here, I kept them as a souvenir. I was thinking of making a collage out of them and putting them on the walls of the salon as a kind of "before and after" display – look.'

The veins on his forehead and nose started twitching and his eyes crossed as he looked at what I'd done with his old election pamphlets. Actually, it had been Starsky's idea for the "after" pictures; he had cut off the top of Mickey's head and replaced it with Eminem's.

'Anyway', Shay was saying; 'you don't want to look too average, or people will think you've got something to hide.'

Mickey looked wild-eyed for a moment; then the anger returned to his face and he spoke slowly through his teeth: 'If I lose this election on account of a bad hairstyle, I'll get my friend in the building society to put up the mortgage rate on this place.'

I snapped back: 'Will he still be your friend if you lose your seat?'

Mickey was looking at me in a strange way, but then another client came in and he had to twist his face into a smile. 'Mrs Murphy, how lovely to see you. How's the foot?'

Mrs Murphy glared at him. 'It's me arm that's twisted by the likes of you. Bleedin blood-suckin politicians.'

If we were good enough for the international rock stars, we were certainly good enough for small-town would-be politicians. But not all the election candidates were convinced of the importance of a good hairstyle. Naturally we were offended when we saw one who really needed us, but didn't seem to know it. 'Willy Tighe',

I said to Shay, showing him a pamphlet which had just been dropped in our letterbox. 'The toupée-thatched daytime telly star. He's recently moved into the neighbourhood.'

'Isn't that the guy who interviews people about their sex lives?' Shay sniggered.

'Yeah – he fancies himself as an Irish version of Jerry Springer but there's nothing sexy about Willy. Someone ought to tell him a thick head is no good without the hair.'

Just then Jason Feeney and Mickey Finn appeared, and you could have cut the atmosphere with a pair of scissors. Mickey sat in silence as we chatted with Jason about wigs and hair in general. 'Mr Justice Calvington is coming in to you to have his wig restyled', Jason was telling us. 'He wants you to make it look like hair that's actually growing out of his head.'

Jason wanted subtle highlights for himself. 'I'd like a colour to match the wig, so I won't look stupid if I forget and put it on backwards.'

'Jason', I wagged my scissors at him. 'I'm going to glue that wig onto your head.'

As soon as he'd left, Mickey Finn breathed out. 'Thank God that little faggot is gone. He's after my seat in more ways than one.'

'Mickey', I said; 'if you think the people of Belgowan are going to turn against Jason because he's gay – which we know he's not because his girlfriend is one of our clients – you'd better save yourself the expense of all those election pamphlets.'

'Anyway', Shay cut in; 'Mrs O'Toole told us the NAG Party is going to put up an anti-gay candidate.' She hadn't, but we were sure that they would.

Mickey went out with a perfect haircut but it did nothing for him with that scowl. 'Maybe we should drop him as a client', I said to Shay. 'We can say we're booked out every time he calls.'

'But we need his influence to keep our mortgage down, don't we?'

'He won't have such power for long, by the way things are going. Who do you think people will vote for if they have a choice between him and Willy Tighe, Irish television's answer to sex? Anyway, he never pays for his trims. And my Dad would save a fortune in the pub.'

Snubbing Councillor Mickey turned out to be a big mistake. We only had to cancel one appointment – and suddenly we were getting calls in the small hours from men with country accents claiming to be from the Revenue Commissioners, who were threatening to come in and audit our books.

Councillor Mickey himself even paid us the odd non-hair-related call, to warn us about the hazards of running a business without enough public liability insurance. 'All you need is one allergic reaction to perming lotion and some unfortunate Hollywood actress's head will swell to the size of her silicone implants – and then I'll be there.' He squinted at us and bared his lower teeth. 'If I lose this election, I'll be spending more time in my day job.' Until then, we had forgotten he was a self-employed solicitor.

He even reminded me that my brother Starsky was well-known to the District Court judge who had recently moved into Belgowan. 'He won't be happy about a drug-pusher's sister running a business on his doorstep. This town has gone upmarket now – it's time we got rid of scum like you.'

Tears stung my eyes. But I didn't cry until we were alone in our little kitchen at the back of the salon. Shay wiped my eyes with his T-shirt, joking: 'I'd better start wearing black T-shirts or you'll have to buy waterproof mascara.'

'Scum like me', I sobbed. 'My family has been in this town since the Vikings. He only came here when his father got transferred from a country village. Old Finbarr Finn was a moneylender as well as a councillor, and the villagers threatened to vote with their feet – and their arms. We should have run the likes of him out of Belgowan but everyone was poor in those days and the councillors used to get us grants. Councillor Mickey got my granny her old age pension. At least, that's what he told us.'

The highlight of Councillor Mickey's revenge was a plague of non-paying customers – people who refused to pay because they claimed they were unhappy with their haircuts and others who were under the impression that we did freebies.

Every day for a week, the salon was flooded with Travellers from the illegal campsite on the motorway. Councillor Mickey popped in on a busy morning to smirk. 'Your friend Jason will enjoy getting his golden locks trimmed in the company of the people who are going to vote for him. And Willy Tighe will probably be delighted to meet his fans – who watch his show on tellies wired up to car batteries.'

Shay and I had nothing against Travellers, but we were losing all our other clients. 'Bleedin snobs', I cried as yet another aspiring real estate agent cancelled her appointment. Father Nick was just short of brandishing his Fworrovski cross at the Travellers.

The celebrities, too, for all their liberal lyrics, were reluctant to have their hair styled with the same brush that had been picking nits out of a travelling child's hair – even when we pointed out that they had originally come from Mrs Uberman's mink coat, which had caught them from her frustrated guide dog.

'It's the coat that should be called Rover', Shay said as we checked Vidal for infestation. 'That thing could take itself for a walk.'

Aunty Geraldine agreed. 'The people who bug me are the filthy rich. They do more travellin than the tinkers and no one complains about them. If they paid their bleedin taxes, the Travellers could have a luxury campsite.'

'Aunty Ger, you couldn't, like, put a hex on them, could you? Just one that would make them go to another salon – or to camp in Councillor Mickey's garden?'

'Kay, lovie, I'm a fortune-teller, not a bleedin gipsy.'

'You could have fooled me with that headscarf.'

'Eh, it's just to protect me hair. You never know where Rover picked up those nits – Mrs Uberman can hardly be expected to keep an eye on him.'

Still, George Morton and Jason stayed loyal – though they came in after hours and Jason, despite his 'open mind', insisted the brushes came directly out of the steriliser). 'I don't want people calling me "Jason of the Golden Fleas."'

The problem solved itself in the end, when Mrs Uberman's coat was attacked with a spray can by local members of Rock Against Fur.

Meanwhile, Councillor Mickey got the Council bailiffs to move the Travellers on because residents were complaining.

'I feel terrible, Shay. Half the celebrities here came from American trailer parks and they all live in caravans when they're filming. We should have done something to help our own Travellers.'

'We can vote for Jason.'

'Thanks', Jason cut in; 'but I've had enough of politics. I don't stand a chance against Willy Tighe anyway. Snobbery will win – one kind or the other. What chance has a leftie politician got in a town where no one will admit to being "working class"?'

Slowly, we got most of our old customers back. But now we had competition: a big international chain, Glamourcuts, was opening a branch around the corner. The manager was our old enemy, Vicky Sheeran.

'Shay, do you think she'll remember us?' I certainly remembered her; the photo smirking at us from the ad in the local paper was the same one that city centre salon had used in the ad to recruit trainees – the ad we had answered. It was the sort of thing Aunty Geraldine had warned us about: 'Beware of destiny', she had said cryptically while she was gazing into her crystal ball (well, that's what she called a tumbler of gin).

'Course Vicky'll remember us', Shay was saying now. 'She'll be dead jealous when she sees what she lost.'

'I suppose this'll be war', I said.

'Nah; the snobs around here won't have anything to do with chain salons. She'll just take some of our middle-class clients.'

But Glamourcuts had a secret weapon: the 'Scissors Wizard', Barbara Burrows called him in her column.

'Shay, look at this.' I showed him the photo of Barbara having her mop trimmed by London's hippest new stylist, Gary Wu. Glamourcuts had paid him an undisclosed sum to move to Ireland. Now his handsome half-Chinese features sneered at us over a caption: 'Gary Wu-es me'. The headline taunted: 'Other hairstylists will "Wu" the day Gary moved in to Ireland's glitziest town.' There was a quote from him in Barbara's article: 'Whoever gave you this cut should stick to mowing the lawn.'

'That's our hairstyle he's chopping', I wailed.

The article got worse. Sniffa Dawg and his harem had been in for makeovers for their new video. Enrico Bendini had hired Gary to do the hair for all the cast in a new film which was being made in Belgowan. Even Linda Morton had popped in for a trim.

'That's a bit strange', Shay said. 'You'd think Gary would want to do something more radical than give her a trim – you know, mark his territory.'

'Well, I suppose he didn't want to change the style. At least one of our cuts got his approval.'

'Yeah. Pity there isn't a photo of Linda in the article. Barbara Burrows is obviously going to give Gary all the good publicity now.'

At least George Morton was still coming to us for cuts. 'How's Linda?' I asked him once, but he just glared at me and said: 'My wife is the same as ever.'

Neil Titwick was reluctant to go back to London without having met his ex-model. 'Linda wouldn't ignore my messages – I'm sure her husband hasn't told her I'm looking for her.'

I looked at him. 'Neil, can I ask you something? If you were crusty old George Morton, would you tell your sexy wife that a famous photographer was looking for her?'

He grinned. 'A gorgeous famous photographer', he corrected me, running his manicured fingers through his new gold highlights.

Neil's talent-scouting sessions in the Ardnarock Hotel suite hadn't thrown up an Irish version of Pamela Anderson, but he was so much in love with the town that he eventually decided to stay. 'I'm going to base myself here and tour Europe', he said. He was buying a penthouse attached to the hotel and planned to stock it with models. 'I'm dedicated to my work', he told us.

The local would-be models – and especially their mothers – went a nice Irish shade of green when Neil's harem started arriving, piece by curvy piece. 'They're all anorexic', the matronly mother of a former Miss Belgowan informed me.

'They have to be; the camera makes everyone look fatter', Shay cut in. He was spending a lot of time at Neil's place, grooming the girls for their photo sessions.

Willy Tighe eventually saw reason and took time off from his doorstep campaign to have a blow-dry. He was smaller than he looked on telly, and pale without the make-up.

'I want it parted exactly here.' He showed us his best side (actually, it was the best of a bad lot). 'And don't use hairspray – I want it moving naturally.'

'Blowing in the wind', Shay hummed and put on the Red Hot Chili Peppers.

'What's that crap?' Willy snapped. 'Haven't you got a TV in this place?'

Shay bit his lip and blow-dried Willy's mat at full speed. When Willy left, Shay pulled out two fags, lit one for each of us and fumed. 'Bleedin wanker. He just wanted to see his own re-runs.'

Jason had come in and was sniggering on the sofa. 'Did youse see his show last night? He was interviewing transvestites at a convention in the Ardnarock Hotel – only he called it the "Ardnafrock" and he called this town "Ardnagowan", and he showed a close-up of the hotel's old ad, which they used to put in *Rare Auld Ireland* magazine: "A TV in every room." The manager is furious.'

Shay turned to me. 'That hotel has potential – for us. All those guys needing temporary extensions.'

'It'll be fun if Willy comes across the Neighbours Against Gays candidate on his doorstep campaign', Jason was chortling. 'You know he's hoping to get the movie stars' votes by projecting a liberal image? He's telling everyone he's bisexual – though his wife swears he's asexual. He's going around in a pink Bentley and he's called his house "Knocknashee" – that's Irish for shaggin' fairies. And he's been doing telly ads for that dating service, the Gay X-change. His slogan is: "Swop your old gay for a new one".'

'Who's the NAG candidate?' I cut in.

'Oh, haven't you heard? Sonny O'Toole.'

'Our landlady's son? I mean, our soon-to-be-ex-landlady's?'

'Yeah – Mr Bachelor Boy himself. Here's his pamphlet.' Jason handed us a fold-up with a daring picture of fifty-year-old Sonny in his Gaelic football kit. 'He only plays bleedin Subbuteo', Jason laughed. Sonny's other hobbies were listed as coin-collecting (which fitted in well with his profession: 'certified accountant') and singing in the church choir (though he didn't mention that Father Nick had replaced the folk group with U2 CDs).

'He's got some nerve, going up for election. It seems he really believes the theory that Jesus was an Irishman because he was thirty-three and still living with his Mammy', Jason said. 'But he's way past the deadline. He's not goin to find any apostles to help him in his election campaign –'

'Unless you count his Ma and her friends', Shay pointed out.

'He's going to have to find a wife and kids and a Labrador retriever – fast', Jason chuckled. 'After all, he's promoting himself as a family values man. One widowed mother just won't cut it.'

I suddenly had an idea. 'Thanks, Jason!' I said, giving him a hug.

'What's that for?' he smiled.

'You've given me an idea: Mrs O'Toole won't evict us if we help her son win the election.'

Jason suddenly looked thoughtful. 'Youse need a Plan B, just in case he doesn't get elected', he said. 'Shay, didn't you tell me youse two had a video of Mrs O'Toole snooping through your personal belongings?'

Shay and I looked at each other. Then Shay turned to Jason: 'Are you thinking of blackmail?'

'Well, yeah, actually.' Jason coloured a bit.

'Cool!' we said.

Sonny O'Toole was a man who didn't welcome change with open arms. After all, he had spent all fifty years of his life dining in his mother's kitchen. Half a century of mushy peas takes the life out of a man. Mr O'Toole Senior had shuffled off after an accident with a rolling pin some twenty years before, so Sonny was the man of the house – and Mrs O'Toole wasn't going to hand him over to 'those brazen Protestant hussies' who worked with him in the venerable Anglo-Irish accountancy firm of Pennyfeather & Worthington.

Even the temptresses on St Ned's church choir were never able to get a spiritual squeeze out of him during the annual religious retreats. 'All that hugging and talking about love – it's not good for you', I used to hear Mrs O'Toole screeching at him when I was a little girl.

Poor Sonny's teenage rebellion started when he was thirty-three and ended after a few weeks, when he realised that it would be hard to find a woman brave enough to take on Mrs O'Toole in a sweeping-brush fight. And one tough woman was enough for him.

But the prospect of having a son on the local council would loosen old Mammy O'Toole's apron strings a bit, we thought, so we approached her with confidence. 'If you let us stay in the bedsit, we'll give Sonny a killer image', Shay told her.

Mrs O'Toole took a lot of convincing. We gave her a copy of the blackmail video. 'I don't know how to use those things', she said.

'Here.' I handed her a set of prints – stills from the video. The best showed her with her nose in Shay's Y-fronts.

She squinted and took her glasses out of her apron pocket. 'Who's that?' she screeched. 'Doris Day?'

I looked at Shay. 'So much for Jason's Plan B', I said. 'Have you got a Plan C?'

So we spent a fortune on bottles of draught stout. Eventually she pursed her lips, wagged her finger and made a deal: 'If he wins the election, I'll waive the interest on your arrears. If he loses, youse are out on your arses.'

'What did she mean about "waving our ears"?' Shay asked me later. 'I'll straighten her face if she goes anywhere near us with her old curling tongs –'

'She wasn't talking about hairdressing, Shay. She was just using some accountants' slang she learned from her son.'

Sonny himself was confident of a 'landslide victory'. The politically correct brigade had had their day, he said, and now it was the turn of 'decent, normal folk'.

'We'll do our best', I said. I wasn't going to promise miracles; there was only so much a scissors could do with a head like Sonny's.

We got him to part with the grey strands that he had plastered over his bald patch, and put a few discreet lowlights in what was left, just to make his hair look healthier (mutton chops for dinner every day for fifty years hadn't produced lustrous locks).

The new look got him a date, in the modest shape of Belgowan's disenfranchised organist, Muriel. 'She's perfect for a politician who wants to look average; she's so ordinary it's weird', I told Shay after we had set the lady's hair in a chic retro wave.

'Yeah – and they'll have plenty in common. They're about the same age, they've never been kissed and they can grumble together about Father Nick.'

Unfortunately for Sonny and the NAG Party, Muriel didn't even make it as far as a cosy photo on his new pamphlet. Sonny told us about it the morning after their date: 'She said honesty was the thing she was looking for in a man, so I admitted I had asked her out because she was perfect for my image – not too flashy. That was when she threw the spaghetti frutta del mare at me.'

'Well, at least you ate something new', I laughed. 'Hey, there'll be other dates – if you let us work on your image, we'll find you a nice fancy woman.'

'After the election', he said. 'I never fancied the Muriel type anyway.'

Dear Mr Duffy,

I am Sunita. I have 19 years, 170 metres and 99-58-95 cm. Here is a photo of me.

I am from Spain but I am in Ireland to study the English language.

I am also a very good hairdresser. My host mother say me you will give me a job.

Thank you. You can find me in the house of Family Keegan: Number Legs 11, Oyster Lane. Telephone Two Fat Ladies, Full House. (I hope I write the numbers properly. Mrs Keegan teach me.) I wait with pleasure for your response.

Sunita Nachos

'I wonder why she addressed it just to you. It's my salon too, you know.'

'Well, it's not my fault, is it? Mrs Keegan – her "host mother" – must have told her I was the boss.'

'The old wagon! She did that to annoy me. Mam said the Keegans never forgave our family since our Bernie beat their twins in the Bonny Baby contest.'

'Well, it's not the Spanish girl's fault. Maybe we should give her a job.' Shay was looking at the full-length photo – I hoped he was just studying the hair.

'Shay, we can't afford staff. We're barely scraping by.'

'But if we had an extra pair of hands, we'd be able to squeeze in a few more clients. We can pay her a trainee's wage and give her all the dirty work.'

In the end, he convinced me that we really needed a Spanish sex-bomb to sweep the floor and scrub heads. We walked around the corner to the Keegan house which was just across from where I used to live. It was the first time I'd actually been on my old street since I'd moved back to Belgowan; I had been avoiding it. Now I felt my eyes brim over as I stared up at my old bedroom window, where Bernie and I had slept in bunks. There were new curtains on the windows – boring beige. Our Mickey Mouse curtains had looked better. There was a yellow sports car parked in the drive – whoever had rent-purchased our house off the Council after us had obviously made a fortune on the resale.

But Mrs Keegan hadn't changed. Her hair still looked like Ronald McDonald's after an accident with a faulty fusebox. The Keegans had always been proud of their curly red locks, and the twins, Mairéad and Sinéad, had spent every Saturday auditioning for child model agencies which specialised in knitwear ads and postcards.

I had often wondered what had happened to them after my family had left Belgowan. Now, as we entered the little sittingroom, I stared at a photo of the pair of them in Irish dancing dresses. The photo was the same one I remembered from the last time I'd been in the house – at their seventh birthday party. It was directly under their First Holy Communion photo. There should have been a photo of them wearing black gowns and mortarboards on top of awful 'nineties neo-hippy hairbeads, or at least gold-plated tiaras and Joint Miss Belgowan sashes (after all, their Aunty Vera had held that title for twenty years – she had refused to tell the organisers where she'd hidden the trophy).

'The girls are in Australia', Mrs Keegan said. She showed me a postcard they had sent her from Sydney.

'Oh, that must be lovely for them', I said.

'It's not – all that sun isn't good for their delicate complexions. That's what ruined their modelling careers, you know. They're teaching Irish dancing over there.' She smirked. 'You know, they were thinking of coming back here to do a hairdressing course and open up their own salon in the town. After all, it's an easy job.'

'Well, why don't they do it then?' I shot back.

'What's that lovely smell?' Shay suddenly asked.

'It must be my cabbage boiling over', Mrs Keegan said and ran into the kitchen. But it wasn't cabbage. It was Sunita.

She stood on the end of the stairs and gazed at my Shay with the same big brown eyes we'd seen in the photo that had been stapled to her CV. I elbowed Shay. 'Shut your gob before someone scores a goal in it.'

'It was the hair I was looking at', Shay was saying to me. It was a Monday morning, Sunita's first day with us, and she was already half an hour late.

'I suppose she's walking slowly in case someone thinks she's carrying the Olympic torch on her head', I snapped. It was easy to see why Mrs Keegan doted on Sunita; she was like two red-headed twins rolled into one. She was even taking Irish dancing lessons one night a week in the church hall from one of the *Riverdance* stars; Sunita's background in flamenco would give her a head start on the others in the National Championships, Mrs Keegan had boasted.

Sunita bounced in around midday, when we were thinking of closing for lunch because business was slack.

'Hello, Séamus', she gushed. I stared at Shay; only his granny called him Séamus. He shrugged at me but he couldn't hide his grin.

'Hello, Mrs Séamus', she said with a flick of her waist-length flames.

'How'ya, Sunita', I said and held out a sweeping brush. 'You can make up for being late by sweeping the path in front of the shop.'

Sunita narrowed her smouldering eyes; she looked like a big tiger, ready to pounce on me. She glanced around at Shay, but he was slinking into the kitchen – chicken, I thought. Sunita took the brush and sashayed out to the pavement, where she spent half an hour doing her best Cinderella impression.

I called her in when I realised that the butcher from across the road was ignoring a queue in his shop to have a conversation in broken English.

'Sunita, would you like to wash Mrs O'Toole's hair?' I said sweetly. Mrs O'Toole had become a loyal customer ever since we had upholstered her Sonny's scalp, but she didn't believe in paying; she obviously thought mopping our landing and binning our packets of condoms were payment enough.

Sunita and Mrs O'Toole smiled at each other. It was the first time I'd ever seen Mrs O'Toole do anything but squint, and the sight of her sunken gums nearly put me off my sandwich. 'Thatsh a lovely girl', she said to Shay and me. 'Whatsh your name, lovie?'

George Morton was even more impressed with our apprentice, who was delighted to chat with him in Spanish.

'I thought it was Portuguese you spoke', I interrupted him. 'Remember you told us that was how you blagged your way onto the judging panel for the Miss Brazil contest and met the winner – your wife.'

'Yes, but these days I find Spanish far more exciting', he said, without taking his eyes off Sunita's cleavage.

Sunita seemed to have an endless wardrobe of body-baring outfits. Our male clients (and Shay) placed bets each morning on which asset she was going to display. 'The legs', Steve Oldman was saying. 'We 'aven't seen 'em for two days.'

'She's probably waiting one more day for the hairs to grow long so she can get them waxed', I cut in. 'Those Latin girls are very hairy.'

'I'd be glad to 'elp 'er shave 'em', Neil Titwick chortled. 'Did I tell you I used to groom my own models?' He was looking forward to photographing Sunita and had even promised us a free poster of her for the salon –'Lady Godivar on an 'Arley Davison'.

I wasn't jealous. Not really; I knew my Shay was only suffering from work stress when he moaned 'Sunita' in his sleep.

'It's all right, love. She's just a lazy lump. I'll sack her tomorrow.'

'No, noooo!' he sobbed.

'Shhh! You'll wake Vidal.'

In the end, it was our female clients who won. They were all mysteriously cancelling appointments – not just for themselves but also on behalf of their husbands. Shay and I took a deep breath as we watched Sunita stuff her last fifty euro tip into her bra; then I took the plunge.

'Sunita, it's just not working out between us.'

'I know', she said with a smile at Shay.

'I mean, between you and us. You're too, well, distracting for our clients.'

Sunita's big eyes filled with tears. I almost felt sorry for her, but it was time to be hard – and Shay would have to agree. 'I'll tell you what', I said to her: 'You can get a job down in Glamourcuts – it's got an even friendlier working environment. We'll put in a word for you with the manager. Vicky was our first boss.' I was thinking: 'Revenge, at last!'

Vicky said yes before she even saw Sunita or her CV (actually, a discreet phone call proved to be the best way to get her to agree to take Sunita). She was desperate for a new apprentice to bully. 'The girls in this town walk out the minute I say "Boo" to them.'

'I know, Vicky. They just don't make apprentice hairdressers like me and Shay any more.'

Our male clients didn't follow Sunita to Glamourcuts; they had obviously already got her number.

Meanwhile, Vicky handled her the professional way – she made her wear a baggy black T-shirt with the 'Glamourcuts' logo across the back, with loose black trousers. 'But I no have the flat shoes', I heard Sunita whinging at Vicky outside

Glamourcuts one morning. 'You must pay me more eef you want me to buy them.'

'I don't care whether you buy Gucci or Thriftytoes', Vicky was snarling. 'If you can't afford them, borrow them!'

'But where can I find someone who has thees kind of shoe? There ees no traffic meter lady in my host family.'

Gary Wu was nowhere to be seen. 'Glamourcuts must keep him locked in a cupboard with the expensive conditioner', I said to Shay.

'I met him in the pub last night while you were watching *Fair City*.' (Shay never likes soaps, so I usually watch them with Vidal curled up on my lap and a box of chocolates.) 'He told me he had called in sick because he had snorted too much cocaine and he couldn't cut hair with blood coming out of his nose; it would look like he'd cut himself with his own scissors. Oh, by the way, he's invited us to a party at his place this weekend. Want to go?'

Of course I did. Gary Wu's parties were supposed to be livelier than Sniffa Dawg's. I left Shay to look after the salon while I went shopping in the city centre with Bernie.

'You're not going to wear that?' Motherhood had turned Bernie into a right little mammy.

I pulled the skirt lower down on my hips to cover my thong and show my navel. 'This is the kind of thing Sniffa Dawg's backing dancers wear in his videos', I said. 'I'll look out of place if I cover myself up.' I found a cute little cropped T-shirt and a pair of zebra-print knee-high boots to go with the outfit.

The Belgowan Residents' Association couldn't bully the likes of Gary Wu into turning down the volume on his sound system. Shay and I clinked cans and toasted Gary for finally bringing those old biddies to heel.

'….so I told Mrs Moran from the 'ouse across the road to turn down her 'earing aid, and then the coppers came and I got Tiffany 'ere to show 'em round the pool', he said.

Gary's penthouse was right next door to Neil Titwick's and they shared a swimming pool which was always well-stocked with man-eating mermaids. Conor, the manager of the Ardnarock Hotel downstairs, was relaxing on a lilo; these days he had no problem finding presentable young waitresses willing to work for the minimum wage.

Sunita was there, of course, gyrating in front of Steve Oldman, who was so stoned he could barely stand up. His wife was on a couch, snogging with Eric Stuntmeyer's wife. The yogis were on the floor, meditating over a big ashtray.

I was surprised to find my brother Starsky there. 'I thought you were back inside', I said.

'Parole', he replied and offered to cut me a line.

'No thanks, Starsky. If Mam finds out you're taking that stuff again, there'll be murder –'

'It's all right, darlin', Gary cut in. 'That's clean, innit? I got it from Sniffa Dawg's dealer, wot used to work for Linda Morton's family back on the plantation – by the way, I didn't steal 'er from you and Shay. Barbara Burrows made that up about 'er coming to me for a trim. I wish she would', he laughed.

'That's strange', I said. 'I wonder who's doing her hair now?'

'She's probably got a live-in hairstylist. She loves 'avin young blokes around. Yo! Pierre – why didn't you bring your mistress to my par'y?'

Pierre was looking a bit deflated, I thought. Linda Morton had obviously found a new toyboy, but Pierre was too proud to admit it. 'I need to take a rest from her – she's exhausting', he was purring.

Javier, Linda's riding instructor, cut in: 'She ees very tired now – we've been galloping all day.'

Gary took us aside; he needed a favour. 'See that bloke over there with the long black ponytail?'

I certainly did – and Shay saw me looking.

'Well, 'e used to work for Linda Morton as a masseur. Then one morning while she was out, George fired 'im – wouldn't even let 'im say goodbye to 'er. The fing is, 'e's also a promising 'airstylist. Got a job immediately at Glamourcuts. But, after 'aving Linda Morton cooing over 'im, the poor bloke can't get used to Vicky yelling at 'im all day to sweep this, wash that. Could you use 'im as an apprentice?'

'We'll think about it', I said before Shay could say yes; he's a big softie.

But we didn't need to think long about it. 'I'd forgotten how tedious sweeping hairs off the floor was', I said as we sat up smoking in bed that night. For all her faults, Sunita had been handy to have around. 'We need someone to boss around', I added, just in case Shay got it into his head to take on another petulant princess.

Shay gave me one of those looks that remind me he's really not so dim. 'Kay, I hope you're not turning into Vicky.'

Lorcan was exactly what we needed: willing to work, talented and well turned-out in a black Gucci turtleneck and Armani jeans. They were real, too; Linda Morton had obviously dressed him as well as she had undressed him.

He had a nice accent, too, which went down well with our social-climbing clients. 'My parents want me to be architects like themselves', he told us. 'They think I take the bus to university every morning. They'd kill me if they saw me working in here.'

We promised to warn him if either of his parents popped in for a hairdo; they lived in Belgowan. 'Dad's more of a barber man, but he's going through his mid-life crisis, so he might just fancy a few highlights to match the new sports car. Mum plays golf; she just gets a short back and sides in the country club salon, but if Dad glams up, she'll do the same; she's very competitive.'

Bigwigs

The local elections were scheduled for the day after Valentine's Day. Sonny O'Toole thought the timing was insensitive. 'If the election was a day earlier, it would save me the price of a meal for two.' He had made it up with Muriel, who, as a bonus, had promised to give all his supporters a lift to the polling station which was in the public library. 'I don't know how she's going to fit all those Zimmer frames in her little car', Sonny said.

Shay and I celebrated Valentine's Day with a meal in Luigi Benvenuto's restaurant, Il Pasticcio. Luigi himself was at the next table holding hands with Charisse, who was wearing one of the dresses from her boutique – with hair by us.

'There's George Morton', I whispered to Shay. 'Is that Sunita with him?'

'Yeah – there's no mistaking that body', he said – then, when he saw my face, he added: 'Or the hair.'

Linda Morton was obviously having a cosy Valentine's evening in. We could only guess who was sharing it with her. It wasn't Pierre or Javier or even Neil Titwick; they were all celebrating at various tables with backing dancers from Jurassic Rox. Sniffa Dawg and his harem were holding court at the centre table; they had a plate in the middle and were sniffing and shaking their heads to the music on the Walkmans Luigi had loaned them, rather than give in to their complaints about his Pavarotti and Andrea Boccelli CDs.

Mickey Finn was sitting in the corner, facing out; his mousy wife, Bridie, was staring past him at the whitewashed wall. They weren't talking. I'd only ever seen her on his election pamphlets, along with his kids and dog. Maybe he hired them for elections.

Jason and his beautiful girlfriend, Valerie, were gazing into each other's eyes and fondling fingers at a discreet table behind a rubber plant. Valerie was one of our favourite clients; her hair was silky and looked good no matter what shade we coloured it. 'I wonder if Jason has discovered yet that she's not a natural blonde?' Shay said.

'I don't think it would matter to a bloke who wears a wig to work.'

Later, we cuddled up in bed with Vidal and talked about our wedding plans; we hadn't even set the date but we knew we'd get around it as soon as we finished that marriage preparation course.

'Shay, do you think Father Nick will make us start from the beginning again? I mean, we've only attended two classes out of the seven they've held.'

'I don't think he even noticed our absence. He was too busy ligging with the celebrity speakers.'

We promised Mickey we'd vote for him as we walked into the polling booth. Mind you, we'd also promised Sonny O'Toole and Willy Tighe, and Jason before he'd pulled out; there wouldn't be enough seats on the Council for all the people we'd promised to vote for. 'Who did you vote for?' I asked Shay as we passed Mickey on the way out (he was ignoring all the people coming out and hugging everyone on the way in).

'I gave Elvis Fox my number one. He's an independent candidate who's campaigning for karaoke bars to be opened late at night. Actually, I voted for him because I like the sideburns. My second preference was for that Al Fayida candidate – you know the guy with the super cool beard who's staying in Sheikh Ahmed's mansion? Deeply religious. Totally honest dude. At least he believes in what he's saying. And he's keen to integrate into Irish culture; he paid a few million for an Irish passport. What about you?'

'Oh, I gave the Totally Real IRA bloke my number one, and after that I gave old Sir Humphrey a vote – the Brits weren't the worst, my granddad used to say. At least they kept the place tidy. Sonny O'Toole was my third preference – well, he wouldn't be normally, but if he gets in, we can tell everyone we did his hair.'

Shay sniggered: 'I think we can do without that kind of publicity.'

'I just hope that Green Party bloke doesn't get in. He's in favour of recycling. I mean, what are we going to do with all the hair on the salon floor? Make it into wigs? He hates hairdressers, if his own hair is anything to go by.'

Shay nodded grimly. Anyone could see that the Green candidate believed in the 'natural look'; his grey hair hung down to the bum of his dirty jeans and he obviously hadn't trimmed his beard since Woodstock.

'You'd think he'd get his hair dyed green to remind everyone of his politics', I said. 'I mean, he's obviously desperate for votes – he got his name legally changed to Diarmuid "Keep Belgowan Common" O'Fogey.'

'Well that was stupid of him. No one around here will vote for anyone called "Common".'

Later that night, we met up with Jason and Valerie, Neil Titwick and his latest 'bird', Gary and another model, and the entire crew of Jurassic Rox with their wives and dancers. We all crammed into the back room of Mental to watch the count on telly; it was safer than facing Councillor Mickey if he lost.

There were seven recounts; Mickey was determined to get in. Eventually his lackeys were able to hoist him up on their shoulders like a big sack of potatoes. They were sweating as much as he was.

Willy Tighe lost spectacularly and made some venomous comments about 'begrudgers' who would have voted for anyone rather than a home-grown celebrity. He also threatened to expose the 'corrupt counting system' on his TV show.

'The biggest surprise was Councillor What's-his-name losing his seat', I heard one of my old neighbours say to another.

'Who?'

'No one ever remembers his name but he's a legend in Belgowan; he used to get all the Alzheimer votes. He's one of the Venerable Grey Men who've been sitting on the Council for generations – since his great-grandfather's time. Actually, most people think he's the same man. But no one has ever had the temerity to ask him.'

Sonny O'Toole, amazingly, scraped in. Mrs O'Toole and her cronies were dancing around him in a circle. 'It looks like some pagan witchcraft ritual', Steve Oldman was saying to his manager. 'Maybe we should get a clip of it for our new video, with some creepy music – it'd be a nice, fresh lead-in to our heavy metal sequence.'

Shay hugged me. 'We won't be homeless after all.'

I wasn't so sure. 'Let's hope Mrs O'Toole doesn't start looking for more upmarket tenants, now that her son's on the local council.'

'Maybe she'll decide mopping the landing is too menial for the mother of a councillor', Shay said. He's always been such an optimist,
God love him.

Mustafa Bin Fahreg, the Al Fayida candidate, went into hiding for a few weeks after the election; two CIA blokes (who had been staying with George Morton to help him with his latest novel) came into the salon to ask if we'd seen him.

'Bleedin cheek of them', Shay said as they drove away in an armoured Merc. 'Comin in here with their shaven heads and expectin us to rat on a potential client. I only hope he hasn't gone away for good; I'm dyin to get my scissors into that beard.'

Sheikh Ahmed was furious. 'My friend had to leave without his wives', he told us as we straightened his moustache. 'Now I've got two sets in my harem and they're all fighting for top position.'

'Isn't he supposed to be the new Bin Laden?' Shay asked.

The Sheikh shrugged. 'How can I have a bin laden in my home when the CIA are rifling through my rubbish every morning?'

Mustafa came back when the CIA had left town. But we didn't recognise him at first.

'Jayz, you must have done something awful to your own people to get a scalping like that', Shay said. 'I thought they were supposed to chop the whole head off. It would have been more bleedin civilised. And what happened to the beard?'

'I had to shave to disguise myself.'

He wanted us to give him something that would make his beard grow back in time for his speech to the faithful, which would be broadcast on satellite TV to strict Muslim countries. 'The Mullahs will put a curse on my head if I appear with a naked face.'

'Over here we curse barefaced politicians', Shay sniggered. 'And "mullahs" – all our geriatric rockers are askin for that style. Bleedin hair-esy.' He glued a long black beard onto Mustafa's chin and trimmed it into a point. 'It's real hair', he told Mustafa.

It was; I had cut off Lorcan's ponytail that morning to help him get a car (his Dad had refused to buy him one because, he claimed, Lorcan's head looked 'like roadkill). Poor Lorcan had asked us to keep the ponytail so he could clip it on whenever his parents weren't with him.

'I'm sure Lorcan won't begrudge it to Mustafa', I said to Shay. 'After all, it's found an appreciative home – and it'll be on TV. Lorcan has often said part of him would like to be famous.'

Barbara Burrows came in just as Mustafa was leaving. She clutched me. 'Isn't that what's-his-name?'

I hesitated, then whispered: 'He used to be in that 'eighties band, ZZ Top. Then his beard fell off and his fans defected to Rolf Harris. But he'll be back in the charts with that beard we gave him. Massive, isn't it?'

The problem with having a celebrity clientele was that everyone wanted to be the prima donna. It wasn't a simple matter of remembering how they took their caffé macchiato or which seat they preferred. Those things were easy to remember; as a general rule, only a has-been or never-has-been wanted to sit in the VIP seat which was right in the centre of the salon, visible from the street – a magnet for autograph-hunters, groupies and gossip columnists such as Barbara Burrows.

No; the real challenge was to keep some harmony in the salon when it was full of mega-large egos – especially as far as the women were concerned. When you've been voted Sexiest Woman in the World by *Playboy* magazine for a decade, it's not easy to sit beside the current winner, who also happens to be tipped for an Oscar and is writing her autobiography. It's hard to look at her photo on the front cover of every magazine in your local hair salon.

'Maybe Linda Morton is staying away to avoid Birgitta Stormberg', I said to Shay. 'I mean, Birgitta is all over the magazines, she's twenty years younger and she's got so much going on in her life, while poor Linda is just buried alive with George.'

Shay sniggered. 'Up to her neck in toyboys, more likely. She's just too busy to come in.'

Birgitta was getting out of her chauffeur-driven black limo in the street. She was handing her poodle to the chauffeur, a handsome Latin type in ripped jeans and a tight black T-shirt which showed off his broad shoulders and biceps. He opened the door of the salon for her, she kissed Bubbles and stood in the doorway, waiting for Shay to show her to her seat. This lady always expected the full service.

She flicked through photos of herself in all the magazines as Shay put her highlights in. It was a top-secret job: Birgitta's agent had threatened to sue us if we revealed that the Swedish sex-bomb was not a natural blonde. We had been especially careful not to book Barbara Burrows in on the same day, and I kept a look-out while mixing the peroxide and ammonia. I put some rollers in the trolley beside Birgitta so it would look as if we were just giving her a set.

'Though I can't see what the fuss is about', I whispered to Shay in the kitchen as we left Birgitta's highlights baking under the drying lamp. 'I mean, the best blondes have always been brunettes underneath: Marilyn Monroe, Brigitte Bardot, Britt Ekland, Madonna, Jerry Hall.'

Shay smiled. 'Well, her secret is bound to get out some day. And, when it does, the world will realise it was all the work of two hairdressing geniuses.'

I gave him a squeeze, stubbed out my ciggie and went back out to the salon.

Now Birgitta was chatting with her agent on a mobile phone. He was more than an agent, by the sound of it. Her whirlwind divorce was still in the news, and her ex-husband wasn't talking to the papers, so this was serious tabloid fodder. I admit we were tempted; we could offer the story to one of the major British or American scandal sheets, who paid decent money. Barbara Burrows would never forgive us, though that wouldn't matter; she had a way of scaring off everyone except wannabees. But disloyalty to a celebrity would mean the end of our careers. Birgitta and her manager might even sue us.

Lorcan had been forced to take a day off; we didn't want any gossip getting back to Linda Morton, just in case he was still seeing her behind George's back.

The only other clients we had booked that day were Sheikh Ahmed's new wives (the ones who hadn't discovered divorce and bellydancing stardom). I just hoped they hadn't got tape recorders hidden under their blue burkhas. They arrived together, in single file, the senior one in front. We showed her to the seat beside Birgitta's while the others chatted on the couch. Shay went across the road to the pub; the only man allowed to look at these ladies was their husband.

Birgitta clicked her mobile phone shut and turned to scrutinise the first wife, who removed the veil and stared boldly back from huge, kohl-rimmed black eyes under strong eyebrows.

'I hope you don't mind my asking', Birgitta said, 'but don't you feel like a prisoner in that?'

The lady smiled and replied in careful English: 'Dressed like this, hidden from the eyes of infidel men, we feel safe.'

Birgitta shook her head. 'It just seems such a waste. You could be movie stars – all of you.'

I said nothing and just did what I was being paid to do; make these ladies even more beautiful for their Sheikh. There were seven of them and each wanted a different shade of henna. Maybe he wanted one for every night of the week.

Lorcan came in just as they were putting their veils back on. Some of the wives panicked and got the veils tangled, and the youngest two giggled. Their chauffeur, who was holding the door of the limo for them, glared at Lorcan as if he was a demon.

Lorcan, however, was busy ogling Birgitta Stormberg, who was pretending not to notice while she checked him out in the mirror.

'I thought we gave you a day off, Lorcan', I said.

'Yeah, thanks. I just came in to hide from my Dad – he's parked outside the bank.'

'Lorcan, what are you going to do when your parents expect to be invited to a graduation ceremony?'

'Ah, that's two years away. I'll have left home by then. Maybe I'll be a hairdresser in Hollywood.'

Barbara Burrows 'wasn't herself', as Mam would say. She wasn't even listening when I told her Lorcan used to work for Linda Morton. She was just staring at the *Daily Sin*. There was a picture on the front page of Stephanie Dunne, the English lady who had written *Hollywood Harlots* and *The Queen of Tarts* – and had still found time to sleep with half the Tory party. I read the article over her shoulder:

> ...The stunning Stephanie Dunne is just 'dunned' by Belgowan, a sleepy little town on the Irish east coast. 'I'm going to base my next blockbusting sizzler there', she said as she crossed her lovely legs provocatively.
>
> Posh Stephanie – who attended Saddlesborough Ladies' College and once dated the Prince of Wales – will bring a bit of class to Belgowan, which, she declares, 'is overrun by jumped-up American trailer trash who can't sing, can't act and can't even speak properly'.

She's staying with her good friend, the Duchess of Straththigh, who is sure to introduce her to all her celebrity friends....

And your super *Daily Sin* will be publishing a weekly social diary written specially for you by Stephanie herself.

'Don't you write for that paper sometimes, Barbara?' I asked, just to wake her up – I was afraid she'd spill her coffee all over her lap.

She put down the paper and the coffee. 'Well, I used to. It's got the same publisher as *Sins on Sunday*, but it's aimed at a lower class of reader.'

'Stephanie Dunne – she's Linda Morton's favourite author', Lorcan was saying. 'George used to go livid whenever he caught her reading those books.'

'No wonder he scowled when I showed him that article about her', I said. 'I thought he'd like to know that another famous author was coming to live in Belgowan.'

'What's George like when he's angry?' Shay asked.

Lorcan's face went bright red; he and Linda must have done something to make George angry, I was thinking. Lorcan was rubbing his forehead now and looking at the floor. 'I've never seen him lose his cool', he was saying. 'But Linda used to tell me things.'

This was giving me the creeps. 'Did he hit her?'

Lorcan rubbed his eyes. 'Not that I know of. I mean, I never saw any bruises on her when I was massaging her. I think it was more verbal abuse. He was always trying to ruin her confidence – he used to say she was stupid, uneducated, an ageing has-been whose modelling days were over and who shouldn't waste money on personal fitness trainers – or hairdressers. Mind you, she didn't take it lying down. She said his books had no sex scenes because he didn't do it anymore. She's going to divorce him, you know.'

'Yeah, we know', I said. 'She told us – in confidence.'

'Gotcha', Lorcan said. 'Only a handful of people know about this: ourselves, Pierre, Javier and Brad, her lawyer. Funny, I met Brad in the pub last night and he was worried about her; said she wasn't answering his calls. He's wary of dropping into the house on spec in case George accuses him of trespassing. Linda used to pretend to George that Brad was only there to talk about her grandfather's will.'

'So she never told George she was planning to divorce him?' I asked.

'Brad warned her not to; he was afraid George would shuffle his bank accounts and leave her with nothing, and then Brad wouldn't get paid.'

'Has she really been bonking Brad?' Shay asked, then shrugged at me: 'I'm just curious.'

Lorcan rolled his eyes and smiled. 'Brad, Pierre, Javier, the postman, the milkman, the dog warden who came to put down George's vicious Rottweiler when it attacked her – everyone except George. I would have been next, only George sacked me first.'

'Oh, man', Shay said and squeezed Lorcan's shoulder.

Getting tangled

My twenty-fourth birthday fell on a Friday, so it was a good excuse to close the shop and take the train to Galway for the weekend. We had never been outside Dublin, unless you counted two weeks every summer in Ibiza, so this was an adventure.

'Are we in the country yet?' Shay asked as the last of the suburbs blurred by.

'Not yet, love. We're still in Dublin, I think – only it's spread into the middle of the country.'

When we saw stone walls and sheep, we knew we were in the real Ireland – tourist Ireland, which you see on postcards. To us, it was a foreign land. There was even a rainbow.

'Jayz, Kay, who permed those sheep?'

'That's not a perm – that's natural frizz, like you get on those itchy polonecks your granny buys you for Christmas.'

'I don't think it's natural, love. Look, that sheep has its initials dyed onto its fur. And there's one with a black face – the farmer must have run out of peroxide. The people are weird in these places.'

'Shay, what's the matter?'

'The bleedin country: it gives me the creeps. Isn't this where Sergeant Rory comes from? And all those litter wardens?'

'Ah, Shay, you won't find that type in the country these days –
they've sent all the worst people to Dublin.'

Still, he relaxed only when we got to Galway city.

We were hoping Mrs O'Toole would have forgotten about the rent by the time we got back; we were supposed to pay her that day but we had convinced ourselves that we really needed a holiday so we could return to work refreshed and make more money. 'We might even get the hotel tariff off our tax', Shay had suggested. 'We can say we were checking out the hairdressing talent in Galway.'

We really enjoyed Galway – especially the lively pubs, which were packed with students from the city's university.

'All those brains and not a decent head among them', Shay snorted as yet another tie-dyed ponytail passed by.

An ad in a hair salon window, 'Models required – free cut and highlights', brought back memories of our apprentice days. 'Look, Shay, that's like my first cut', I said as a girl with a crooked fringe came out, arguing with a younger girl who was brandishing a scissors and wailing: 'But it's *meant* to be asymmetrical'.

I looked at Shay. 'We've come a long way.'

'Let's get married', he said. 'Next week.'

We've always believed in doing things quickly. Life is too short for waiting. So we had no rehearsal, no guest list (just a few mobile phone text messages and e-mails to everyone we wanted to invite – and a few we had to) and no wedding list. That's why we ended up with forty toasters (Alessi and Guzzini from our wealthy clients; Pricebuster from everyone else) and the entire contents of the One Euro Shop.

'Do you think this bathmat from your Aunty Sharon will be OK in the bed-living room?' I asked Shay the night before our wedding.

'Well, I suppose it kind of matches the carpet – you can't go wrong with neon pink polyester on orange acrylic. It'll cover that ciggie burn that Mrs O'Toole's always nagging us about. Anyway we haven't got a bath.'

Vidal whimpered. 'Shut up or you'll end up with green fur and then I won't let you be my flower-dog', I warned him. I was showering the dye off his coat; a subtle minty tint would look stunning with the garland of orchids we planned to put around his neck. One of our clients, a florist, was donating the flowers.

I made sure to tell George Morton that I had enough flowers; I was terrified he'd give me a 'bouquet' of dead pheasants. He had given us a card, but it was blank inside.

'I suppose he thought Linda had signed it and she thought he had', Shay said.

Charisse had given me a discount on the wedding dress and bridesmaid's dresses for Bernie and Roz. Roz had promised to do my make-up; she had qualified as a beautician and was thinking of packing in her job in a Ballyskanger salon to go freelance. 'I'm sick of working for other people. They give me all the manky jobs – pedicures, bikini-waxings and blackhead removal.' Shay and I were going to think about offering her a chair in our salon – after the wedding.

Father Nick had slotted us in between the First Holy Communion ceremony (a glamorous occasion, judging by the kiddie bookings at both our place and the tanning salon) and an ecumenical service with the Reverend Vernon Good – who was also insisting on co-preaching at our wedding. Father Nick gave in because the Reverend promised to include the ceremony in his TV show which would be broadcast to the United States. Naturally (or unnaturally, if you were in the know), we had upholstered the Reverend's toupée especially for the occasion.

'Shay, isn't this exciting?'
'Course it is – our last night living in sin.'

It was only a five-minute walk to the church, and for once it wasn't raining, but Steve Oldman had insisted on loaning us his limo and chauffeur. The band was recording in London but they had promised to pop back for the reception, which we were holding in Il Pasticcio – courtesy of Luigi.

'Maybe we should have sold the photo rights to *Hello* or *OK* magazine', I said to Shay as I saw Barbara Burrows and a few other Irish hacks casing the congregation, brandishing tiny tape recorders.

Shay kissed my hand. 'We'll make more money this way – all that local publicity is good for business.'

I looked at him as if he was a gorgeous stranger I'd just met. His short hair had been freshly gelled into twisted spikes. I had trimmed and bleached it myself that morning while I was waiting for my own highlights to take; I had read in *Hair Today* magazine that men fantasised about blondes, had fun with redheads and married brunettes – so I was covering all possibilities by putting three different shades in my hair. I was wearing a veil only because Mam had insisted. 'Mam, veils are for brides with split ends', I had told her.

Shay was in a steel grey suit (denim, with bootleg trousers) and an open-necked shirt. Good old Pierre had loaned him the clothes he'd worn at his job interview with Linda Morton (Pierre had never needed them after that).

Neil Titwick snapped us as we got out of the limo. 'Hold it *jussst* like that – perfect. A little more leg, baby.' I flashed the blue Marks'n'Sparks garter Roz had bought me.

Mam and Dad were getting out of Steve's other limo. Mam was wearing one of Charisse's 'Mother of the Bride' suits with a matching yellow hat. Dad was in his wedding suit, which he wears for all weddings – he's very proud of the fact that he can still fit into it, though Mam always points out 'Your father has had that beer belly since he was sixteen.'

Bernie had decided peach was not her colour after all, and had changed into a black leather mini and mesh top. She had been acting strange lately; Mam thought she might be envious because Fergal, the father of baby Robbie, didn't want to marry her. Still, he had come to the wedding – the two of them were getting off his scooter, looking a bit bedraggled after the long, windy ride from Ballyskanger. Robbie was crying to be let out of Bernie's backpack. 'Not until you clean up that puke!' she was warning him. 'Now, give your Aunty Kay a kiss!'

Starsky surprised us all by arriving on time and showing no signs of having inhaled or injected anything. He had gelled back his hair and was wearing a purple velvet suit he had picked up in a city centre flea market. Some young girls in designer jeans and capped teeth surrounded him in the church car park and pleaded with him for his autograph; he gave them an illegible scribble and walked briskly into the church with Shay.

'Hey, you, bride-thingy!' one of the girls asked me: 'Do you know who that was?'

'Of course I do', I laughed.

'Well, would you mind telling us?'

Dad took my arm. 'I'm delighted to be giving you away at last', he said.

Muriel was thumping out *Ave Maria* on the old organ. She was hitting wrong notes as usual, but I was glad to hear her; it was all very well for rock stars to hold concerts in the church, but I was a Belgowan girl to the core and I wanted a local person to play for my wedding. There was no singer because Sniffa Dawg had offered and, rather than admit rap wasn't my taste in wedding music, I had told him Muriel had gone against the idea. 'She's old and crotchety. She might have a heart attack if we don't do things her way', I said.

Father Nick, two curates and the Reverend Vernon Good (bursting out of a shiny blue suit) were waiting patiently; I was taking my time in those platform sandals. It was funny seeing Shay and his brother Barry on their knees at the altar rail. Barry was holding Vidal – who was yelping and wriggling. Barry made the big mistake of squeezing him and got the sleeve of his rented jacket ripped off. Vidal fell to the floor and ran down the aisle to me. I picked him up and he tried to lick my face through my veil. I didn't mind; the distraction calmed my nerves.

Now Shay was grinning and winking at me. 'You're nearly there, Missus', he whispered. Poor Barry was fumbling in his pocket for the ring while trying to hold the torn elbow of his sleeve close to his side.

The Reverend Vernon Good gave a long boring speech about holy matrimony and lots of religious stuff.

'The Lawd has put these two fahn young people together and only the Lawd – or a lawyer – can separate them', he said.

Father Nick was standing behind the Reverend, looking at his shiny blue bum and shifting from one foot to the other, the way he does when he plays striker on the parish football team.

'I know marriage is supposed to be forever', I whispered to Shay, 'but does the bleedin wedding have to last an eternity?'

Salvation came when the Reverend's gospel choir turned up unexpectedly (much to the annoyance of Sniffa Dog who, judging by his frown, clearly thought we had snubbed him in favour of them – we'd have to give him free extensions to make up for that) and began to sing, their voluminous blue Kaftans swaying to the rhythm, candles in their hands. The Reverend, grinning at the nearest TV camera, was bopping alongside them – and his toupée was keeping the beat, bouncing on his head like the lid on a pedal bin.

I nudged Shay with my elbow. 'Look – it's just hanging on by a piece of sticky tape.'

Then one of the singers jived a little too vigorously and knocked over the big lady next to her – and they all fell down like dominoes. Their candles were flying everywhere. Shay grabbed me, just saving my veil from going on fire.

But the Lawd wasn't looking after the Reverend's toupée; it burst into fire and, for probably the first time in his life, he had luxurious flaming locks.

Father Nick tried to snag the blazing bush with a brass candlestick, but the Reverend Vernon screamed and held it on, scorching his hands as well as his head. Then the two curates grabbed the Reverend, carried him over to the baptismal font and dunked his head in it. There was a sizzle and then silence as the now bald and badly burned preacher turned to face the congregation.

'Jayz, he looks like your man from *Friday the Thirteenth* – the twentieth sequel', Shay sniggered.

The Reverend glared at him, then put his toasted hand into the water, fished out the singed toupée and plonked it back on his bonce. It looked like a Brillo pad. He joined his hands and stared into the camera, which his TV team had wheeled up to the altar.

'Ah have been saved', he said. 'Praise the Lawd.'

The gospel singers started up again: 'Praise the Lawd. Praise the Lawd....'

When they finally stopped, Father Nick rolled his eyes up to Heaven and muttered a few prayers. 'God give me patience. Save me from breaking the Fifth Commandment.'

Then he got to the good bit: 'Do you, Katherine Mary O'Head –'

'It's O'Hare', I said.

'Oh, what's the difference? Do you, Katherine Shay O'Shave – I mean Katherine Mary O'Hare – take this man, Séamus Anthony Duffy, to be your lawful wedded husband.' Except it came out as 'your awful-headed has-been' in Father Nick's new plummy accent. And the only people who ever called me Katherine were my schoolteachers (when I was behaving; when I was bold, they used to call me 'Miss O'Hare!').

'Look, do you want to marry him or not?'

I answered with my best smile. 'Course I do.'

'Praise the Lawd', the Reverend interrupted, but Father Nick just shot him a glare and continued.

I answered 'I do' to each question, except 'for richer – and for poorer', when Father Nick cocked an eyebrow, George Clooney-style, and I replied: 'We've had enough of that' and everyone laughed.

There was a bit of a fuss when Vidal nearly swallowed the ring, but Shay finally got it out of Vidal's throat and on to my finger. It had cost us a whole week's takings but it was worth every cent.

Father Nick flashed his Fworrovski-studded teeth. 'Now you may kiss the bride'.

'As if I needed to be told', Shay said, and gave me a discreet peck on the lips (I'd warned him about messing up my lipstick, and anyway we'd save the passionate stuff for later, without all our relatives looking on).

'Ah go on, give her a good oul' snog!' Shay's Uncle Noel shouted. We found ourselves giggling. 'Not in front of the dog', I yelled back and we ran down the aisle into a hail of confetti. We didn't mind that it was only white aeroboard the butcher had broken up for us, nor that it looked like dandruff. If this was 'for poorer', we knew we'd enjoy the 'for richer' bit.

We stood on the steps for a few more photos. It had started to rain, and Shay's father's black hair dye was running down his face, but we didn't care; we were Mr and Mrs Duffy, hairdressers to the rich and famous.

The Duchess of Straththigh came up to us and kissed us both on the cheeks. She was an elderly lady with vivid red hair and a wicked gleam in her eye. 'I've heard your hair salon is the place where all the beautiful people go', she said.

'Not enough of them', Shay grinned. 'Come into us and we'll sort out that dye.'

She giggled and pinched his cheek. 'Oh, you naughty boy. I certainly shall pay you a visit – with my good friend, Stephanie.' She pulled a glamorous forty-something blonde over by the hand.

'Did you say I was good? Well, well, that's news to me', Stephanie said with a wry smile. 'Hello. Nice to meet you both. I'm that awful author you've been reading about.' She kissed us.

Neil Titwick was snapping us from different angles. 'Stephanie, love, can you look this way? Kay, lean forward a bit – more. Pull the neckline down a bit. Perfect. Bernie, can you come over 'ere? A bit more midriff, love. Gorgeous!'

Barbara Burrows tried to get into the picture, but the Duchess and Stephanie kept standing in front of her.

I threw my bouquet to Roz, who was still looking for Mr Right (any old rock star would do), but Vidal leapt from my arms and fetched it. I let him savage the flowers; if he left a plop on the floor of Luigi's restaurant, at least it would smell nice.

Luigi was waiting for us in Il Pasticcio's elegant dining room. He knelt in front of me, kissed my hand and looked up at me with his bold brown eyes. *'Signora* Dahffee', he said solemnly. Then he grinned and leapt to his feet. 'I 'ave worked all night on theess menu. I 'ope you weell enjoy eet.'

He had decorated the tables with orange flowers and little trays of chocolates which we nibbled while we waited for the starter. It was lobster – and, thanks to Macker, everyone knew the exact location where it had been found. 'About twenty metres down, on a rock bed out where the new sewage pipe ends', he was roaring into the ear of the Duchess of Straththigh. She was giggling; I bet she'd never met the likes of Macker before. Macker's wife was tugging at his sleeve, trying to get him to shut up, but he hadn't put on his best suit and hoovered his beard just so he could sit quietly in a corner.

George Morton was at a table with some of Shay's parents' neighbours. He was just staring into space. I was going to go over and ask him about Linda, but Barbara Burrows beat me to it. 'Linda is fine', I heard him say. 'She couldn't get back from New York in time for the wedding. She's visiting a lady friend.'

'That's odd', Barbara murmured to Neil Titwick. 'She must have slipped out of the country quietly. Either that or she's given the security men at Dublin airport a bigger tip than I do.'

'You know what I find even odder?' he replied. 'She's never *'ad* any female friends. It's somefing I've always found sad.'

I looked around to find Roz; I was suddenly glad to have her as my best friend, even though we hadn't stayed in touch very much since I'd moved away from Ballyskanger. Roz was being chatted up by one of Sniffa Dawg's beefy bodyguards; she gave me the thumbs up behind her back.

We were all sitting down and Barry was staggering to his feet to give a toast when the doors burst open and Luigi's head waiter flew backwards into a bowl of punch. Aunty Geraldine staggered in on her stiletto heels. Her hair was a dishevelled haystack and her mascara had run halfway down her cheeks. She wore a skin-tight pink dress with an indecently low neckline, slit to the hip to show ripped black stockings. She carried a bottle of champagne in her hand – it had a bow on it, so I guessed it was our wedding present, but it was half-empty.

'Whersh my lickle pet? Ah, there you are, lovie! Tell us, when's the babby due?' She threw her arms out in front of her and aimed herself at the head table where I was trying to hide behind the wedding cake. Vidal caught her just in time, darting under the table and grabbing her ankle. She screamed and landed just short of the cake, probably breaking a few teeth (not that that would make much difference to a woman whose speech was permanently slurred).

Everyone stood up and stared at her, except Mam, who vaulted over the table and dragged her up by the hair. 'Jaysus, Geraldine, you're in an awful state', she said, mopping the blood off her face with a linen napkin. But Aunty Geraldine was more concerned about the smashed bottle of champagne. 'What a wayshte', she was mumbling.

'She was exactly the same at our wedding', her husband, Uncle Benjy, was muttering into his champagne. He had got there an hour before her but was avoiding eye contact with her. I guessed he was reminiscing about their own wedding back in the Scary 'Seventies. Bernie and I used to flick through their photo album whenever we got bored watching re-runs of *Hammer House of Horror*. Aunty Geraldine had worn shiny blue eyeshadow and plastic flowers in her waistlength brown hair (that was before she'd discovered peroxide). Uncle

Benjy had worn his ginger mop shoulder-length, with a beard and sideburns flowing out over the pointy collar of his white Abba suit.

The day before our wedding, we had tried to sort out her image with a nice, feathered crop and subtle burgundy tones, but the radically different hairstyle made her look even more like herself; those wild green eyes and fiercely plucked eyebrows were staring at us out of a different frame. It was eerie.

Now Mam and Bernie were leading her off to the Ladies' to be cleaned up, while Luigi tried to hold back the waiter, who was shaking his fist at her.

Then George Morton clapped. Everyone stared at him for a few seconds, before joining him. 'Marvellous', I heard the Duchess say. 'Jolly sporting of them to have a typical Irish drunk at their wedding.'

'I'm just waiting for the fight scene', I heard a Hollywood stunt man say to his wife, who drawled: 'Oh, please, honey, not without the insurance.'

I smiled at Shay. He nuzzled my ear and handed me the knife to cut our cake. 'Thanks be to Jaysus Luigi didn't let your parents mess with it', he said. Mam and Dad are serious sci-fi fans and had been trying to persuade Luigi's chef to replace the little bride and groom with plastic figurines of Mr Spock and Uhura from the original series of *Star Trek* on it.

'Yeah', I said. 'I mean what's wrong with Marge and Homer Simpson?'

After the meal, Sniffa Dawg climbed up on to a table and began rapping: 'The bride is in da house....' He was stomping his trainers which looked cool with the penguin-cut pin-striped trousers and matching jacket he had had tailored in Miami specially for the wedding. His hair had been shaved (I decided we'd have to have a word with him about that; with his lightbulb-shaped head, he needed hair – and so did his hairstylists). His drummer kept time with dessert spoons, and a trio of sexy dancers in belly tops and mini-skirts took the floor.

Jurassic Rox arrived just when Sniffa and his dancers were getting tired and Elvis Fox (who had gate-crashed the reception) was about to get up. Steve Oldman was magnificently decked out in a skin-tight leopard-print suit with a white frilly shirt and he had a streaked, frizzy ponytail (he was hedging his bets, on the advice of his new manager, who wanted him to appeal to three generations of fans).

He kissed me on both cheeks, squeezed Shay's shoulders and yelled to one of his roadies, who threw him the mike. Eric Stuntmeyer plugged in his guitar and bounded up onto the table beside Steve, the backing dancers adjusted their leather mini-skirts and we all sang along to a classic track from the 'eighties. Aunty Geraldine was gyrating in front of Steve and he stooped down to pull her up by the hand – but he hadn't pumped iron for centuries, and she hadn't been to Flab Fighters since they'd upped the fees and changed the name to Absolutely Flabulous, so he fell on top of her.

Neil Titwick captured the moment on camera. 'Magic', he was saying. 'Not since the 'sixties 'ave I seen such debauchery.'

Aunty Geraldine shoved Steve aside and blinked at Neil. 'Were you at my wedding?' she asked.

Our honeymoon was the best reason we could think of for skiving off work (anyway, when you're the proprietor, sickies aren't fun). We left our clients in Lorcan's hands and Vidal with my parents while we flew off to Italy. We were spending two weeks in Luigi's hotel, Il Vecchione, in the Italian seaside town of Macellario.

'That's funny, Shay: I thought the Italians would all be wearing designer clothes, like Luigi.'

'You know what I find stranger? There's no bleedin chipper in this town.'

'That's 'cos these people look after their figures. Luigi told me they ran Massimo out of Italy.'

'It was really good of Luigi to give us a free honeymoon', Shay said as we struggled with the wooden shutters. Eventually we got them open – one came off in my hands. I stepped out onto the balcony. 'Careful!' Shay yelled as part of the crumbly old masonry fell away.

'I just wanted to admire the view', I said, looking out at the rooftops of the old town centre. Well, I could just about make them out in the distance. And there was the sea behind them. I looked down at the bright narrow street full of shops with neon signs and middle-aged men chatting up girls in thigh-high boots and peroxide hair.

'Hey, Shay, this is where the Italian fashion designers get all the ideas for their shows. I just knew Luigi came from a glamorous place.'

There was a lively street carnival going on – scooters crashing, lots of hand-waving and miming and those lovely Italian voices saying things that sounded like the names of flowers but were probably something else, judging by the hand signals.

We heard a bang at our door (actually there was a lot of banging going on in this hotel, by the sounds of it) and an elegant lady with huge brown eyes and even bigger dyed chestnut hair peeped round. 'Good morning. I am Emmanuela. I am the *Mamma* of Luigi. I am so 'appy to meet you. Luigi say me you are a most romantic couple.'

We decided to forget about hair during our honeymoon. We also avoided the Irish pubs where tourists were drinking green beer and singing songs about the IRA. 'Just think, Shay, if we were back in Ireland, we'd be doing green hair-dyes today for the St Patrick's Day parade and giving the Irish dancing contestants frizzy red perms.'

'And insulting all the mega rock stars by filling the town with "sham rock".'

For the first time since were carefree teenagers, we were just chilling out (as our American clients would say). I had fun with the Italian phrases Luigi had taught me – not all of them polite, judging by the locals' reaction – which was usually laughter. But Shay warned me to stick to English. 'I'm sure you learned the wrong name for salami, love.'

Over the next two weeks, we spent a lot of time eating ice-cream in a cliff-top café outside the town. It took two bus rides to get there but it was worth it for the view. The little cliffs of Belgowan and the grey Irish Sea seemed farther away than ever – and, for the first time, I didn't care. I closed my eyes and took off my shades, to let the March sun warm my eyelids. I could get used to blue skies and warm breezes.

'You know, Shay, I'd be happy to live here if we ever lost our salon back in Belgowan', I said.

'We're not going to lose the salon', he said. 'Ever.' He hugged me. 'We'll make lots of money and we'll come here every year for two weeks. Maybe three times a year – hey, maybe we can buy a second home here.'

I cried when we hugged Emmanuela goodbye. 'You will come back. I'm sure of it', she said, crying herself.

Sticky gel

My parents met us at the airport – with Vidal, who went ballistic when he saw us. Dad was his usual talkative self, but Mam seemed to be on edge. 'Are you OK, Mam?' I asked her more than once as she scraped the gears in the Zit. 'I'm fine!' she snapped each time. They gave us the key of our bedsit and drove off. Dad looked puzzled; Mam was hatchet-faced.

'Well, the place looks cleaner than it was before we left', I said as we came in (though I suppose it couldn't have got any dirtier).

Vidal went about the important doggy business of sniffing every piece of furniture to make sure no strangers had been there. Mrs O'Toole didn't count; we were certain she had been in a few times – and now she was banging on our door, asking for the rent.

'Jayz, we haven't even had time to sit down', Shay said to me as he took out his wallet.

Mrs O'Toole asked us what we had done on our honeymoon. 'As if we'd tell her!' Shay snorted after he had closed the door. 'Now, Mrs Duffy, are you ready to do your wifely duty?'

I giggled as he carried me into the bedroom and flung me onto our bed, which Mam had covered with a new bedspread. It smelt nice and clean – almost as nice as Shay, who had poured half a bottle of Italian aftershave over himself to hide the smell of sweat from sleeping in airport lounges.

'Oh, Shay, I forgot to take the pill. We'll have to use the johnnies.'

'No probs. Where are they? In the holdall?'

'I can't remember. I don't feel like unpacking now. Just get some out of the bathroom cabinet.' We had hidden them behind the first aid box in case Mrs O'Toole found them again – or, worse, my mother.

'I can't find them, love. Are you sure you put them here?'

'Let me look. I know where I put them. What's a baby's bottle doing in our cabinet, Shay?'

'How would I know? Maybe your Mam was babysitting little Robbie when she came out to check on the bedsit – Jayz! No wonder she was in a bad humour.'

I was thinking: What did my mother think we were doing, Shay and I, all this time we were shacked up together? Twiddling our thumbs? 'I can't believe she's not speaking to us', I said to Shay.

'She'll be back to her old self after a few days. Let's enjoy the silence while we can. Soon enough she'll be nagging you to give her a grandchild – and then another.'

Shay was right. Mam never could stay away for long. A few days later, she was on the phone, inviting us to Sunday dinner. And yes, she did hint that I should be preparing myself for a new career as a baby factory. 'Youse can't live in a bedsit now that youse are starting a family', she began as soon as we had sat at the table. 'Why don't youse sell that salon and open up in the shopping centre over here – the houses are cheaper and youse could get a mortgage on a nice little three-bedroomer.'

'Mam, we're not ready to have children.'

She dropped her fork. 'What do you mean, lovie? I was younger than you when I had Starsky.'

Exactly, I was thinking, but I said: 'Well, Vidal is enough for us for the moment.'

Mam was looking to Dad for support, but he was having a coughing fit and heading for the bathroom; Dad hates being dragged into arguments, especially when he has no strong feelings on either side. Mam sniffed and we sat in silence for about five minutes as she ladled Brussels sprouts onto all our plates. I hate Brussels sprouts, partly because I hate anything that's good for me but also because that's what my family eat on Sundays – and we always have rows at the table on Sundays.

'Marriage is there for a reason, you know', Mam was going on as she balanced my little nephew, Robbie, on her lap and tried to force-feed him a mashed up mixture of Brussels sprouts and marrowfat peas (no wonder the kid was so flatulent).

'Bernie didn't seem to be too pushed about it', I snapped, and then wished I hadn't; Bernie was like a fuse waiting to be lit these days, and I knew Mam would repeat what I'd said the minute Bernie got home from her date with Fergal.

'That's enough!' Mam said. 'Your sister only made one mistake.'

Is that what you call little Robbie? I was thinking as he burbled green gunge all over Mam's jumper.

'Anyway', Mam was going on, 'Bernie and Fergal are getting married as soon as the Pope gives him an annulment. He was married in a Protestant church before, so that doesn't count as a proper wedding.'

'Now I've heard it all', Shay laughed as we walked to the bus stop. 'Your Bernie is a dark horse, isn't she? And who would have thought Fergal would have had a wife? I wonder if he has to give her half his dole money. Isn't he still living with his parents?'

'I bet Linda Morton doesn't care about not having children', Roz said to me as we saw George getting out of his car. 'She's got her toyboys and George picks up her bills. What more could she want?'

'A more cheerful husband?' I laughed. I hadn't told Roz the gossip about the Morton's upcoming divorce because I firmly believed in the hairdressers' code of conduct. Rule One was: Never give away clients' secrets.

Roz was spending the day as our in-salon beautician; if all went well, she was going to hire a chair from us one day a week. Today, however, she had promised to give us ten per cent of anything she made – which, judging by the takings, would be two euro and fifteen cents. She knew we'd never ask her for it.

Just as Roz was losing hope, Stephanie Dunne came in and asked for a facial. 'Give it a good old pummelling', she was saying as Roz massaged a facial scrub into her forehead. 'I'll be having everything lifted next month anyway. I just want to go on to that operating table looking good.' She gave Roz a fifty euro tip – more than the price of the facial.

She also entertained us with a few horror stories about her experiences with cosmetic surgery. 'Stephanie', Shay said, 'the likes of George Morton can sneer all he wants to about your romantic books, but I think you're braver than all his action heroes put together.'

When Stephanie had driven off, we let Lorcan and Roz go, and waited for our least-favourite after-hours client, George Morton. 'You know what George's problem is?' I said to Shay. 'He never opens up and tells you things, the way Stephanie does. He's too reserved. No wonder his wife doesn't fancy him.'

'She must have fancied him once', Shay said. 'Jayz, let's promise ourselves we'll never get like them.'

'Or my parents.'

'Or mine.'

'Or Bernie and Fergal, or Sergeant Rory and Councillor Mickey Finn and their wives, or —'

Shay shut me up with a passionate snog, which ended only when we heard a loud 'Ahem' from George Morton. For once, he was smiling.

He was back to his talkative self, but without the boasting. 'Isn't it wonderful to be young and in love? I remember when I first met Linda – of course, only she was young, but the passion I felt was as strong as a young man's....' He went on to describe their first meeting, their wedding day – everything but the most intimate details of their marriage.

I raised an eyebrow at Shay. He crossed his eyes at me in the mirror. I tried not to snigger as I trimmed George's hair; he might think I was laughing at him. 'What's so amusing, young lady?' he was asking but I was shaking too much to answer. Once Shay gets me started, I
can't stop.

'I wonder why people confide in their hairdressers', I said to Shay later as we lay in bed with Vidal at our feet. 'I mean, for all they know, we could be telling half of Belgowan.'

'I suppose they know we wouldn't – otherwise Barbara Burrows would have some seriously juicy gossip in her column.'

'But, Shay, don't you think it's kind of, well, flattering that all these rich and famous people tell their secrets to two —'

'Common hairdressers?'

'Shay, I don't mean that.'

'But it's true. We're two lower-class people from Dublin and our clients are just slumming, as I believe it's called.'

I looked into his eyes; they were dull for once. He went on: 'They also confide in other common people – their cleaning ladies, chauffeurs, gardeners, the guy who runs errands for them, their dogs. They tell us things because we're not important enough to keep secrets from. It's like the way they talk in front of waiters; if they were worried about being overheard, they'd eat at home.'

'Shay, do you really believe that?' I felt as if all the colour had been drained out of my little hairdressing world. We were no longer Kay and Shay Duffy, hairdressers to the stars, but simply an ordinary couple who happened to cut hair for a living.

Shay pulled me closer and I lay my cheek on his chest, which had been waxed like an Italian stud's and smelt of that aftershave he'd bought on our honeymoon. 'I'm just telling you how I think they see us. What really matters is the way we see ourselves.'

He kissed the top of my head. 'You, Kay – Mrs Duffy – are the most important person in my life. Anyway, I don't fancy George Morton or Steve Oldman.'

'Or Cameron Diaz?'

'Eh, well – ah, Kay, you've nothing to fear from the likes of her. Natural blondes are no fun for hairdressers.'

A hairy tale

The grocer's in Belgowan attracted three basic kinds of customer:
1.   Thirty-something working mothers with mortgage-stressed faces
and designer-clad kids who were embarrassed to be seen with them in front of their pals from the crèche. They bought frozen ready-made meals and brand-name fizzy drinks for the kids.
2.   Die-hard Belgowan residents who hadn't taken the bait and sold
up to live in Ballyskanger or Clonbollard. These were mostly OAPs. They bought tinned beans and small cuts of meat and grumbled about the prices to the cashiers, who commiserated with them when the manager wasn't there.
3.   The kind of girls you would see hanging around Formula One
pits. They bought nothing but shampoo and shower gel. They spent most of the time casing the gourmet aisle in the hope of spotting a divorced millionaire who hadn't availed of the home-delivery service.

I just didn't fit in there – and neither did George Morton. But there I was, wincing at the prices and wishing I hadn't been too lazy to take the bus out to the cheap supermarket on the outskirts, when I saw George rummaging among the packets of smoked salmon. His trolley was full of frozen chips and ready-made meals for one. No wonder he had put on weight if that was all he was eating. He didn't even notice me – though I suppose that was because I was darting down another aisle.

Later, I told Shay, who just shrugged and said: 'He's probably sacked the errand boy for giving Mrs Morton too much service.'

I saw George Morton in other unusual locations over the next few weeks.

One Sunday at dawn, Shay and I spotted him sitting on the cliff looking out to sea. We had been to a party in Steve Oldman's mansion, and Steve's chauffeur was too stoned to bring us home. It was April and, for once, it wasn't raining, but George had a face like the proverbial wet weekend, so we decided not to say hello. 'He's probably thinking about the plot for his next novel; it would be a shame to disturb him', I   told Shay, who didn't need convincing.

We were sitting in the back row of Belgowan's little cinema one Friday night, when we noticed George in an aisle seat halfway down — which, as anyone who goes to the cinema to actually watch a film knows, is the right place to sit, because the speakers are on the walls at either side.

We were just avoiding Mrs O'Toole, who had developed an annoying habit of calling for the rent at night when we were in the middle of our own love scene.

Anyway, we sat up when we saw George, who was the only other person there apart from the usher (most people in Belgowan these days have their own private cinemas – come to think of it, most of them are in the films).

It was a Jim Carrey film, which definitely didn't seem like George's taste in movies. He must have been interpreting it in some arty-farty Freudian way, because he was actually crying. Either that, or he just didn't like the movie.

Another time, I saw him going into the church. Out of nosiness, I followed him – at a discreet distance. He was on the pew outside the Confessional for about fifteen minutes. I watched from behind the abstract statue of Father Nick (which looked like Quasimodo after a round with Mike Tyson; it had been commissioned by the Duchess of Straththigh and made by some Greek guy who, according to the Duchess, had muscles in all the right places for a sculptor, so Father Nick didn't dare complain).

When the Confessional door opened and Father Nick's voice called out 'Next, please', George seemed to lose his nerve; he went pale and stumbled out of the side-door, while Mrs O'Toole hobbled from the Confessional, muttering prayers to herself – or maybe they were curses, judging by her expression. She and Father Nick don't look at religion in the same way – and he has often confessed to Shay that Mrs O'Toole is 'penance personified'.

'Maybe George is thinking of converting to Catholicism, like the Duchess of Straththigh', I said to Shay.

'Funny you should say that, because, this morning, while I was trimming his beard, he was asking me all about Confession. I told him I wasn't the sort of Catholic who went to Confession and Mass and all that – just the kind who got married in a Catholic church. Anyway, he said he'd heard that a Catholic priest would "never break the seal of the Confession".'

'Well, I hope someone points that out to Father Nick. Mrs O'Toole said he gave a long sermon last Sunday about the lessons we should learn from "a former Hollywood vice queen", "a twice-divorced aristocrat" and "a chart-topping death metal singer with a criminal past" who have all recently converted to Catholicism.'

'Kay, I think it's time we started going to Mass.'

George was visiting *us* more often, too. When he got his beard trimmed for the seventh time in a week, I put down my scissors. 'George, there's no growth to trim, unless you want me to shave it off. Are you just coming in here for the company?'

I'll never forget what happened next. He put his face in his hands and started to cry. He was gasping and sobbing like a little boy, with snot streaming down his chin (except in George's case it was getting stuck in his beard, which was a shame because I'd only just trimmed it). I didn't know what to do or say, so I just patted his head. 'There, there', I said the way Mam had soothed little Robbie after he'd seen her in her slimy green anti-wrinkle face pack.

'What have you done to him, Kay?' Shay was running out with the first aid kit. 'Did you get ammonia in his eyes?'

'Not this time, Shay. I did nothing.'

George was wiping his eyes and blinking at us. He looked worse than my Dad looks with a hangover. Worse even than Starsky when he's having withdrawal symptoms (that's why he just stays on the heroin these days).

'George', I said in my sympathetic voice (which I'd copied from that nice Joan Rivers on American TV): 'You can tell us. Whatever it is, you can trust us.'

He sat up straight and breathed in. 'All right', he sighed. 'I murdered her.'

'Who?' we asked together.

'The Iraqi spy lady?' I suggested.

'No', Shay cut in. 'The American ambassador's wife, isn't it? That bitch you've had in all your novels.'

'I murdered –' He looked at Shay first, then me; his eyes seemed to have lost their colour and shine (not that they were ever sparkling). 'I murdered Linda.'

We stared at him. I thought he was joking. Shay even sniggered and said: 'Yeah, right!' But George was speaking in a monotone. 'I shot her through the left temple as she slept on the chaise longue. She was still flushed from her lovemaking with Pierre or Javier or one of the others – I don't keep track of them any more.... It was a clean death – no screaming, hardly any blood. I cleaned it up myself after I had fed her to Cuddles – that's one of our Rottweilers. Linda always gives the dogs such ridiculous names.'

George's eyebrows shrugged but his eyes were blurred. He continued in the same monotone: 'Well, I'd forgotten how fond of Linda Cuddles was. He licked the bones and growled when I tried to take them back. I watched him as he buried the bones in different places – it was quite touching, really. Of course, I couldn't risk the gardener finding them, so as soon as Cuddles had finished and was safely chained up in his kennel, I dug them up myself and tried to grind them down in my paper-shredder — wrecked the thing. Had to throw it out, as a matter of fact. It's probably being turned into tin cans at the Council's recycling plant at this very moment. Think about that the next time you drink a can of cola.'

He haw-hawed; we just stared.

He went on: 'In any case, it didn't damage the bones; just stripped off the gunge that was stuck to them. So I wrapped them in a black plastic bin liner and forgot about them for the night. The next morning, I borrowed Macker's boat – I often do that when I'm working on the plot in one of my thrillers. Macker lets me; he's not a morning person.'

That was true; Macker usually surfaced around noon with a hangover. But I still wasn't sure about the rest of George's story.

'Sometimes, I drop the fish traps for him. I just fill them up with the bait he keeps in a big plastic box on deck and leave them in the usual places, which he's got marked on his chart in the cabin. Anyway, I knew there would be a few empty traps on board because I'd seen him haul them in the previous day, so I just picked a good sturdy one and stuffed the bin liner with the bones in it into that; it took me two minutes max. No one was around to see me; the people who live around here are a lazy lot, aren't they? Steve Oldman's mansion looks out over the harbour but as far as I could see, all the curtains were closed.'

I nodded. Steve had been terrified of the dawn ever since his lawyers lost a libel action against the *Morning Sun* for 'irreparable damage' to his public image.

Now George's eyes were brimming with tears, but he continued to speak in that dead tone.

'I took her far out, way past that sewage outflow where he usually drops his traps, and rolled the trap over the side of the boat. I put an extra lead weight in just to make sure it would go straight down. It did –
with a splash, thanks to the plastic bag inside.... My wife always was a sloppy diver.' Now a tear rolled down his left cheek.

We still didn't know whether or not to believe him, but we shuddered at the thought of Mrs Morton lying on the seabed off Belgowan – the bits of her that Cuddles hadn't had for lunch. She had always been terrified of Cuddles; he was the only one of George's Rottweilers she hadn't been able to convert to vegetarianism. After this, we'd give up eating fish.

Shay grabbed George by the shoulders and looked into his red-rimmed eyes. 'Do you mind if we ask you a few questions?'

'Not at all', George sighed, looking steadily at Shay now. 'It will be a relief to talk. Shoot.'

'OK. Why are you telling us?'

George hesitated, then a crooked grin spread across his fishy lips. 'Because it's therapeutic to talk – and because I know you won't tell anyone. You're hairdressers: you never reveal clients' secrets.'

'Try us', I cut in.

He turned to fix me with his dull eyes. 'Who'll believe you, if you don't believe me? There's no body. No one knows where Linda is – or where she's supposed to be. She's estranged from her family. She's got no friends, only young men who use her for her beautiful body, her body which is now – which is no longer –' He collapsed into another sobbing fit.

Well, now we were beginning to think that he might be telling a 'nonfiction' (as I suppose he'd call it). As if in a dream, I brushed the hairs off his beard while Shay took the money.

George sobbed 'I'll be back for another trim' and waved at us – a limp flip of his big, murdering hand – as he shuffled out with his head down.

I looked at Shay and burst into tears. 'I hope Cuddles gets indigestion from Mrs Morton's silicone implants and the vet turns out to be a vivisectionist.'

Shay pulled my face onto his T-shirt. I felt his tears on my forehead, but his voice was calm: 'Kay, let's go to the cops.'

I was still crying, but I found myself agreeing with George. 'They won't believe us, Shay.' I tried to imagine Sergeant Rory or his like listening to us, and all I could see was a sneering face under a peaked cap. 'Wasting police time', they would say. They might even have us charged with it.

Sniffa Dawg was rapping on the radio; something about wanting to stab a policeman. Now we no longer felt like dancing to it.

Split ends

'She's writing a novel', Pierre was telling me as I trimmed his hair.

'Was she – is she?'

'Yes. She showed me the first draft. It's not my kind of novel – more a woman's read, the kind secretaries hide under their desks and are ashamed to be caught reading. I'm sure it will be a bestseller; after all, she's writing about what she knows. It will be – how do you say it? – a bonkbuster.' He puffed out his chest. Pierre was proud of his English slang. 'She's got a name for it already: "*A Bomb in His Briefs*." She's going to write it under a pen-name, of course. She's fed up with fame.'

'Why's that?' I found myself asking; I expected him to say she was hiding from a stalker.

Pierre shrugged. 'She told me she didn't want reporters interviewing her ex-boyfriends back as far as high school.'

'When was the last time you saw her, Pierre?'

'Oh, I don't keep track of these things. I see her whenever I have the time.' But his face was turning red. He added: 'I think she's out of the country. She's probably visiting friends – doing some more research for her novel.'

'Maybe she's visiting her family in Sao Paolo?'

'No. Absolutely not. She doesn't want anything to do with them. They're criminals, you see.'

Javier too was still pretending he was seeing Linda. 'I spent every night last week with her', he boasted to Shay in the pub.

Brad, true to his profession, was availing of the right to silence. I held the scissors just centimetres from his eyes, and asked him how Mrs Morton was and how her divorce was going, but each time he looked at the floor and said: 'Hey, what's this? An inquest?'

'There's nothing we can do', Shay said as we lay in bed. We had smoked two packets of fags and still hadn't found a solution. 'She's dead and nothing is going to bring her back. No one will believe George Morton killed her – not without evidence. He'll be let off and he'll probably write a best-selling novel about it.'

'The scumbag!'

'And if we talk about it, he'll sue us for slander. We'll lose our salon. We'll never be able to afford our own home – and Vidal won't have a garden.'

Vidal whimpered and wriggled up between us to lick our faces.

We thought about turning George away the next time he called in for a beard trim and deep conditioning treatment. 'What he needs', I waved my scissors at Shay, 'is not a hairdresser – but a taxidermist.'

We were more than disgusted; we feared for our own safety and Vidal's. After all, George was capable of murdering us too if he put his mind to it. We had watched enough films to realise that cold-blooded murderers have no sense of honour – and, according to the *Sunday Times* book critic: 'George Morton knows all there is to know about murder'.

But we needed the money. Business wasn't good enough to choose our customers on moral grounds – or fear. Anyway, I decided we'd try to get him to go to the cops voluntarily.

'George, we've been thinking, Shay and I, that it must be a terrible strain on you, knowing you, well, murdered Linda –' I choked back a sob and ran into the kitchen to wipe my eyes. Shay came in after me with my mascara wand. 'Come on, love, don't fall to pieces. It won't help Linda – oh, Kay!' We hugged and I could feel Shay's tears in my hair, even through the leave-in conditioner.

George was calmly reading a magazine when we came out: *Vogue*. There was a feature on the world's one hundred most beautiful women, and Linda was among them. The photo had been taken by Neil Titwick for a 1985 lingerie calendar. Linda looked slimmer in the body (it was before she'd had the bust op) and plumper in the face (the nose hadn't yet been pared away by cosmetic surgery and cocaine). There was a quote from Neil: 'She had the elegance of Christie

Brinkley and the sex appeal of Madonna. She was conscious of the effect she had on men, but too shy to exploit it to the max.'

'That was the year I fell in love with her', George said. 'She played the part of an ingenuous South American spy in the film adaptation of my novel, *The Colombian Connection*.'

'Yeah, you told us', I cut in, but he wasn't listening.

'It took me five years to approach her for a date', he was murmuring. 'She said no twice. Then one night she called me. Her latest lover had cleaned out her bank account. Her film had been a flop. She had no prospects. She didn't actually say all that. All she said was: "Yes". So I gave her a diamond engagement ring.'

'Why didn't her family come to the wedding?' I felt entitled to ask him anything now; after all, he had burdened us with a secret that was keeping us awake every night.

'You know they're a major drug dynasty?'

'Yeah, but since when has that got in the way of family weddings?'

George's eyes seemed to be looking inwards. 'Linda was different. She was a really moral person – I know you find that hard to believe, in Catholic Ireland, but adultery isn't the worst sin.'

'Murder is', I said, watching him in the mirror. Shay put a hand on my shoulder.

George just gazed at the magazine picture of Linda. After a long pause, he murmured: 'I wanted her to stay like that.'

Sonny O'Toole was looking pleased with himself – and he wanted everyone to know why. He insisted on planting copies of the *Residents' Association Newsletter* all over our salon. I took them away the minute he'd left; the last thing you wanted to see as you sat under the drier was a photocopied photo of his big round face and baldy head. It was a charity that the Residents' Association could afford only a black-and-white copier. I looked at the headline: 'Dogs to be muzzled at all times.' Inside was a report of the local council meeting, at which Councillor Sonny O'Toole had secured a majority vote for tough dog control laws. According to him, Belgowan's 'wealthy residents are liable to sue the Council if they are bitten on a public street'.

'Shay, have you seen this? We can't bring Vidal outside the bedsit without a muzzle.'

'Jayz, Kay, can you see Vidal in a muzzle? He'll go mental.'

'We'll have to just bring him out at night and hope no one sees us, until we can afford a car to take him out of town.'

'But, Kay, I thought we were saving up for a home mortgage – so we can have a house with a garden for him to play in.'

'Maybe we should just move somewhere else. I mean, Belgowan is turning into an obstacle course. If it isn't stupid old Councillor Sonny, it's his old witch of a mother threatening to put up the rent, or Councillor Mickey threatening to sue us for not paying our Chamber of Commerce fees, or Sergeant Rory giving our clients parking tickets because he says there are double yellow lines under the tarmac outside our shop.'

'Or George Morton coming to give us our daily dose of the creeps', Shay said and pulled me to him. He nuzzled my forehead – but it was like being rubbed with sandpaper.

'Shay, you forgot to shave under your nose – for the second day running.'

'Eh, I'm growin a Freddie Mercury.'

Now I was worried about him. Shay had never worn a moustache before; he'd always said they were only for master butchers and those women who complain about their haircuts.

'Are you all right, love?' I caressed the stubble. It went out as far as his ears! 'Shay, don't you think this is a bit ambitious? I mean, I'm sure even Freddie Mercury started with something modest.'

'Nah, I'm goin to grow a *most*-ache, like this.' He showed me a Muzzgrows catalogue, *Ready-to-Wear Facial Hair*. 'See, Kay, they're all the rage. Course, I'd rather grow my own 'cos you never know where they got these – they claim to use real hair.'

'Shay, I know what you're like. You won't stop until you look like a bleedin Bandito.' I flicked through the colour booklet. 'Ugh! It says this Hitler Moustache is the real thing.'

'Just goes to show you how hairstyles have evolved. He'd never have become a dictator with that little toothbrush job these days – even Saddam Hussein's wasn't big enough to keep him in power.'

'Shay, you're a hairdresser, not a bleedin dictator. Look, why don't you go for this style?'

'The Starter Muss? That's for fairies. Errol bleedin Flynn had that and he used to wear tights.'

'So did Freddie Mercury.' I turned the page. 'How about this one? The Lounge Lizard.'

'That's only for pimps and porn stars.'

'Well, the Seán Connery, then? Look, they have it advertised with matching eyebrows.'

'No bleedin way! That'd make me look like an Army bloke – a poxy English Major. That's what George Morton says he was when he was our age.'

'He couldn't have been, Shay. He was at university – in America. That just goes to show you what a liar he is.'

Shay gave me a forced smile – the kind that goes with a moustache. 'Bet you've never snogged a bloke with a muss.'

'I don't want a hair sandwich.'

'I promise to keep it groomed. I fancy a waxed moustache – Roz can wax it for me.'

'It's supposed to be more painful than a bikini-wax – and anyway it's only for women.'

He kissed my fingers. 'That's why I'm getting it done; for my woman. It'll be my Latin Lover look – to go with that aftershave I bought in Macellario. Hey, Kay, let's just leave Lorcan in charge again and go over there for another two weeks. We need a holiday. Luigi says we can stay in his Mamma's hotel anytime, free.'

'We can't afford the plane fare.'

'We can get a cheap flight to Rome on the internet, then take the train down to Macellario. It'll be cool.'

I sighed. It was tempting, but I knew that if we spent one more week in Italy, we'd never come back to Belgowan, our landlady, our local politicians and police and, especially, George Morton.

The strain was making us snap at each other. Shay is normally so laid back that he doesn't even complain when I use his last disposable razor to shave my legs, or wash his favourite pale shirts with my black trousers. His sunniness is one of the reasons I love him; he cheers me up even when I've got bad PMT. But now everything I did was irritating him. 'Kay, I'm trying to watch the telly. Do you have to hum?'

'There's a right hum off those underpants you left on the bed', I shot back.

'Right. I'll just do the housework and you can watch bleedin MTV. I mean, it's not as if the Ireland versus France match is important, anyway.'

'Why don't you go down the pub and watch it with the other drunks? It'd save me clearing up the beer cans.'

'Right. I'm goin to the bleedin pub. If I see George Morton, I'll buy him a drink – he knows how to deal with naggin wives.'

I burst into tears. I knew he didn't mean it, but my nerves were getting the better of me and I couldn't see a way out. Shay pulled me into his arms. I cried onto the bit of his chest that was exposed by his open-neck shirt. I was glad he'd let the hairs grow back; they were part of him and I needed as much of my Shay as possible (though I still wasn't keen on the idea of a mega-muss; I had nightmares about waking up beside a 'seventies TV detective or, worse, George Morton).

Vidal was whimpering at our ankles and doing the tango with his hind legs. 'He wants to do a wee', I said. 'You carry him under your anorak and I'll go ahead to make sure Sonny or Mrs O'Toole aren't around.'

Dark grey roots

'Here, Shay, it says in this book that you can grind bones in a paper-shredder.'

I showed him *Murder in Miami* by George Morton, which had a yellow 'Bestseller' sticker on it.

'Yeah, maybe that's what he was thinking about when he said he tried it', Shay said. 'But it doesn't mean he actually did it. He's got a wild imagination, you know.'

'Shay, why would he say he killed his wife? Just for a joke?'

Shay shrugged. 'I don't know, love. Maybe he's got a weird sense of humour. Those literary types are strange.' He was flicking through another of George's novels. 'Jayz, Kay, I'd love to be a character in one of these – a psychotic hairdresser who goes ape-shit with a pair of scissors and some perming acid.'

'Shay, love, don't get any ideas; we need those clients.'

Jason was sitting innocently beside George Morton one day, when I got an idea. 'Jason', I said, 'you know something about the law, don't you?'

'I bleedin should', he laughed. 'Why?'

'Well, since you're a successful barrister', I said loudly, 'as well as being a moral person –'

'Well, thanks. I don't know if I deserve –'

'Shut up and listen to me!'

'Okay, okay. Jayz, Kay, relax.'

'Sorry Jason. I just want you to solve a problem – one that doesn't actually exist.'

'All right: a hypothetical problem. I'll do my best.'

'Well, here goes. What would you do if someone told you – in confidence – that they had committed a crime, and you had no evidence, and the cops wouldn't take you seriously even if you told them.'

Jason was wearing that 'Have you been drinking?' look I'd often seen people give my Aunty Geraldine.

'Jason, it's just a question – for a moral dilemma quiz I'm taking part in, in the pub.'

He perked up. 'That sounds like a lively evening. I love getting into moral dilemmas. When's it happening?'

'It's not in Belgowan. It's out in Ballyskanger. You wouldn't like it – it's a rough area, and anyway I mightn't take part.'

'Oh, okay then. Well, my answer as a lawyer is that you can't accuse someone of a crime if you've got no evidence. But morally, you'd be obliged to check it out – find out if the person is telling you the truth or just having you on.'

George Morton had been pretending to read *Style* all that time (or maybe he really was interested in that feature on fashion for larger ladies). But now I noticed he was sniggering. I left poor Jason with half his head trimmed and ran into the kitchen to wipe my eyes.

'Maybe Jason has a point', Shay said later. 'Maybe we should check out George's story ourselves. After all, making up stories is what he does for a living. How do we know Linda hasn't simply, well –'

'Disappeared? Ah, come on, Shay. She would have told us.'

To: info@freshfaces.com
From: uglyhairstudio@iol.ie
Date: 10 May 2001
    Dear Sir/Madam,

We would like to know if you are the Fresh Faces model agency in California who gave Linda Mata (now Mrs Morton) her big break (see last month's issue of *Vogue*: 'The World's Top One Hundred Most Beautiful Women').

If you are, we hope you won't mind helping us. We are trying to find out if dandruff runs in her family. This is very important for the welfare of her hair, as well as her future career prospects. She wants to make a comeback and looks even more beautiful than she did in the 'eighties; only her chronic dandruff is holding her back.

As we're sure you will appreciate, this is a delicate matter that we can't mention to Mrs Morton or her current husband, the famous writer George Morton.' You can contact us at the above email address.

    Yours sincerely,
    Kay and Shay Duffy

To: uglyhairstudio@iol.ie
    From: Suzy.Mata@riorestaurant.com
    Date: 11 May 2001.

    Dear Kay and Shay,

Alan Couch at Fresh Faces model agency told me you were looking for information about my sister's dandruff problem. I am surprised; Linda has always had healthy hair, as has everyone else in our family.

However, we would like to know how she is. She hasn't been in touch for eight years. She never answers our letters and we haven't got her phone number. We weren't even invited to her wedding.   Frankly,   we   are

worried about her. She has always been emotionally unstable – could this be causing her dandruff?
　　Can I ask you to do me a favour? If I fly over in a week or two, can you arrange for me to bump into her in the local bar?
Please consider it. You would be doing Linda a big favour.
　　Can you recommend a nice hotel?
　　Sincerely,
　　Suzy Mata

Suzy Mata had the same brown eyes and black eyebrows as Linda, but she was more pitbull than sex-siren. Her clothes were what you'd call conservative; they were the kind of clothes our middle-class clients wore. But what bothered me most was the hair: whoever had put that henna in it was her worst enemy.

I was surprised when I heard her accent; it was pure Californian, from what I knew about accents (with so many Hollywood stars in Belgowan, it was becoming common). She stroke confidently across the salon in her leather court shoes, sat down in our VIP chair, crossed one trouser-suited leg over the other, took out an elegant silver cigarette case and brandished a slim cigarette.

'No thanks', I said, though I was dying for a smoke. I wished Shay would hurry back from the bank. This woman was making me nervous – and I couldn't figure out why.

'So, you know my sister', she was saying, fixing me with those ferrety brown eyes which seemed to be boring holes into my own. 'I must say, I'm happy to find that she's got a female friend, at last. You're more than just her hairdresser, right?'

'Yes. We're her friends – my husband and I. Here he is now. Shay, this is Linda's sister, Suzy Mata.'

'Her twin sister', Suzy added with a smile. 'Isn't it obvious?'

Shay raised an eyebrow at me, then turned to Suzy. 'How's it goin?' He shook her hand.

'Pleased to meet you', she said, giving him a matter-of-fact handshake.

She was happy to talk about Linda. In fact, she was determined to make us listen. Half an hour later, she was still yackering on. 'When Linda was a little girl, nothing was too good for her: piano lessons, horse-riding, ballet tuition at the best dance academy in L.A., voice coaching to lose the accent – it's funny to think that she puts it on now –, the most expensive clothes.'

I remembered something Neil Titwick had told us: Linda never had dates when she was a teenager. 'Her parents fort she was too good for the neighbourhood blokes. They just saved 'er up like an investment. Linda was going to make 'em proud someday. She was going to be a successful professional something or other and marry a nice, well-brought up type with a secure income and membership of the country club.'

Now, listening to Suzy Mata, I guessed that it hadn't been an unreasonable ambition for a second-generation immigrant Brazilian couple to have their beautiful, bright daughter live the American dream for them – and to ignore her twin. Poor Suzy had obviously inherited all the bad genes.

'Linda was far too good to work in our family restaurant', she said. 'She was going to be our parents' reward for all that hard work. I guess they'll have to wait for the next life.'

She dragged on the cigarette, puckering her lips, which had been severely lined to make them look fuller but failed.

'Did she have any other sisters or brothers?'

'No. Just me. But she was like lots of children rolled into one.' Suzy blew smoke at the mirror. 'First she was a promising pianist, then some teacher said she was so good at biology, she'd become a surgeon.... In high school, she was top of her class in everything – writing, painting, science projects. We were in the same class, and I suppose I was a disappointment to the teachers. She failed at only one thing in school: dating. She was always getting hit on by guys, but she brushed them off. She seemed to be holding out for someone better.' Suzy giggled. 'The other girls in our grade said she was the oldest virgin in California. She didn't go to her prom because she didn't have a date.'

Suzy blew another cloud of smoke and went on: 'In our final year of high school, she won the Young Filmmaker of the Year award and for a while she was pitching scripts at all the studios. The studios sent them back with notes saying she was "promising". Linda was always "promising".' Suzy drawled out the word: 'praw-missing'.

Linda certainly wasn't praw-missing now, I wanted to say. After all, dead was about as unsuccessful as you could get; murdered even worse.

But Shay and I had only the word of a fiction-writer to go on –
a man who told lies for a living. We were still hoping that the murder had been a figment of George's sick imagination, so we didn't tell her twin.

Now Suzy was sighing, and great clouds of sweet-scented smoke were coming out of her. 'Linda changed when she went to university. Maybe it was because she was living away from home – in an apartment paid for by us, her hardworking family, from the takings I counted every night in the restaurant. Anyway, she let us down, big time – partied all through her first year at university, then dropped out. That was when she won the Miss Brazil contest.'

Suzy stopped to light another cigarette, stubbing out the used one in her coffee cup. She waved the ciggie at me in the mirror. 'Linda wouldn't have got a job, even if she had managed to graduate; she was only doing an arts degree. She convinced our parents that she had so many options, she needed to keep them open. She was going to follow it up with a Masters in something or other – she hadn't decided what.

'After she dropped out, she moved in with some photographer, an English guy –'

'Neil Titwick?' I bit my lip too late.

'Yeah. She told you, I suppose. He launched her as a model. Suddenly, she didn't want to know us – anyway, we were scandalised by those photos. I just think it's so tacky. No self-respecting woman would do it.' She sniffed. 'Well, she got tired of Neil as soon as she found a more useful boyfriend: Doctor Vanitoso. I'm sure you've heard of him.'

'The name sounds familiar.' Now did I say that? It wasn't as if he was right in front of me, expecting to be well-known. Still, you couldn't be too careful in a town full of celebrities.

'He's famous for breast implants – other people's.' She haw-hawed at her own joke. 'Y'know, California is full of anorexic ex-prom queens working in diners and gas stations to pay off the mortgage on their double F cups.

'After her second op, she left him for Max Spozya, the producer. You've heard of him, of course.'

Shay shook his head. 'No, love, we haven't – though I'm sure he'll buy a house here sooner or later.'

Suzy frowned. 'Why do all these celebrities want to live in middle-of-nowhere-burg?'

'Tax incentives', I said. 'And to escape their relatives. Only the most persistent ones would follow them here.'

'So, Suzy', Shay cut in, 'do you have anyone else in your life?'

Suzy snorted, took another drag of her ciggie and blew a smoke cloud. 'The usual: ex-husband, twin girls.' She sighed. 'Mom and Pop never noticed me until I gave them grandkids. Now I'm the favourite daughter. They don't mention Linda so much these days. I wonder what would happen if she came back home.'

'Family life was always a big turn-off for Linda', George was saying as I massaged his scalp. 'She never wanted children – said pregnancy would ruin her figure. And she hated it when I had my relatives to visit.'

'George, did she ever have any of her own family to visit?' Even though I knew the answer, I was curious to hear his take on Suzy.

He cocked an eyebrow. 'Never. She didn't get on with them – didn't even invite them to our wedding, which my people thought was most odd. She said they would ruin everything. I was so in love with her, I just accepted it. I didn't really believe that they were drug barons, but I humoured her because it appealed to her sense of drama.'

He sighed. 'Anyway she burst into tears whenever I suggested having them over. I only met them once, briefly, and that was at her aunt's funeral.'

'What were they like?'

'Well, her parents were civil to me, but reserved – that's only natural at a funeral. Her twin sister – Suzy – was making a big effort to put me at ease. I was grateful for that, so I commented that she could be mistaken for Linda if she grew her hair – well, there were other differences, but I could hardly say that. Anyway, Linda got very tense, so we left as soon as the aunt was buried.'

He shrugged. 'I tried to get her to make peace with her family. After all, her parents only wanted the best for her. And as for her sister – well, Linda's intelligent enough to realise how hard it must have been for Suzy, growing up with a twin everyone adored, being compared with her, trying to squeeze into her hand-me-downs.'

'George, would you like to meet Suzy again – now?'

He turned around to face me. 'What? Now that Linda's dead? Now that I've, well, murdered her.' His eyes filled with tears but he was still staring at me.

'George, I don't believe you killed her.' I still wasn't sure.

'You don't? You think I'm such a sick joker?' The tears were running down into his beard now. He looked at me through blurry eyes. 'You think I'm incapable of committing a crime I write about in all my novels?'

Now was not the moment to tell him Linda's twin sister was in town.

'Her twin sister? Yes, I remember she mentioned her', Brad said. He had finally admitted that he hadn't a clue where his client was (actually, he only admitted it when I had his head rigged up to an electric scalp stimulator with the power turned up to 'maXXX'). Now he was fishing for news of her – and I was meting out the bait.

'She didn't get on well with her twin, did she?' I asked, giving him my best innocent look.

Brad smirked as if he was proud to be the expert on Linda Morton. 'Linda told me Suzy had always resented her.' He made a comic pout and squeaked in a bad imitation of Linda's voice: '"She's like a little dog, always snapping at my heels".' He sniggered. 'Linda didn't even want Suzy at her wedding in case she put a hex on it. She said Suzy used to pretend to be her and try to seduce her boyfriends – and when that didn't work, she started introducing them to other women. Either Suzy is one sick chick or Linda is paranoid.'

'Suzy will be delighted when George and Linda divorce', I suggested.

Brad sniggered again. 'Well, at least she can't do any harm to that relationship. George and Linda are the most divorce-able couple I've ever had the pleasure of unhitching.'

'Brad, would you like to meet Suzy?'

'Well, sure, yeah, I suppose so.' He shrugged. 'Hey, maybe we'll bump into each other if she turns up to gloat during the divorce hearing. It'll be in all the papers anyway: "'Eighties sex symbol divorces best-selling author".

'Well, here she is – look.'

Brad spun around, pulling all the wires out of the scalp-stimulator; he looked weird with wires growing from little circular pads on his head. Suzy, of course, stared right back.

I broke the ice. 'Suzy, how are you today? Never mind – this is a friend of Linda's.' Suzy's mouth formed an 'O'. 'Brad, this is Suzy Mata, Linda Morton's sister.' Brad gaped.

'Her twin sister', I added. Brad gaped even more.

There was silence for a moment. Then Suzy spoke. 'Nice to meet you', she said, holding out her painted claws. 'What did you say your name was?'

'Brad. Brad Fisher.' He shook hands briefly, then folded his arms.

'Well, the name suits – the Brad bit. You look kinda like Brad Pitt.' She giggled, a girly little sound that didn't go with her pebbly brown eyes.

Brad shrugged but didn't smile. He kept his arms folded.

Suzy sat down in the swivel-chair next to Brad's, and they looked at each other in the big mirror. She held a cigarette out to Brad, who waved it away. She put it between her gungy orange lipsticked lips, lit it, inhaled and blew smoke at Brad's reflection. 'So, Brad, you know Linda.'

'You could say that.'

'Have you seen her lately?'

Brad smiled and rolled his eyes up to the ceiling. He sighed. 'Last time would have been, um, a month ago. She had me for lunch.' He was grinning now, fighting the urge to laugh and losing the battle.

Suzy turned to blow smoke in his direction. She frowned.

Brad sat up straight, the way my Dad does at the bar when he's trying to convince the barman to give him 'one lasht pint'. 'I'm sorry', he said, 'I don't know where Linda is. When was the last time you were in contact with her?'

'Eight years ago.'

'May I ask why you need to see her?' Suzy stiffened but Brad shrugged. 'Hey, don't take offence. I'm just offering to pass a message on – if I come across her, that is. I can't guarantee I'll see her; she gets around a bit, you know.'

Suzy's eyes filled with tears. 'I just want to know where she is', she said, her voice shaking. 'It's not knowing that makes me angr – sad.'

Suzy snapped open her handbag and pulled out a biro and card. She scribbled something, then shoved the card at Brad, who took it with his fingertips. 'I've written down the number of the hotel where I'm staying. If you hear anything, I'd appreciate a call.'

She got up and headed towards the door, then spun round to look back at Brad: 'And if you'd like to have dinner, well....' Brad was just staring blankly at her. She waggled her fingers, then stalked out.

Instead of running after her, I crossed out her appointment.

Brad leaned back in the chair and looked up at me. 'Hard to believe she's Linda's twin', he said and put the card in his pocket.

'Will you tell her if Linda contacts you?'

He shook his head. 'My duty is to my client.'

Later, in bed, I cried on Shay's chest. 'Our duty is to our client too. What if George really has murdered her?'

Shay laughed that shaky laugh that he always has in moments of crisis: 'Well, if she's dead, she's not our client. But George still is. And we can't break his confidence – anyway, if he has killed her, nothing is going to bring her back.'

'Do you really believe he's telling the truth, Shay?' I asked for the zillionth time.

'No, 'course I don't. Well, I hope he's not. Maybe he's trying out a new plot for one of his thrillers. After all, if you can get two cynical Dubliners like us to believe it, you can fool tens of thousands of readers around the world.'

'I hope you're right.' I rubbed my face in his chest – which felt different, somehow. I switched on the light. '*Shay*! Your chest hair!'

He looked sheepish – literally. 'I just wanted to test that new batch of peroxide.'

We were relieved when the manager of the Ardnarock Hotel told us Suzy Mata had booked out. So was he. 'I came closer to turning into Basil Fawlty than at any time in my career', he told us as we covered over his grey hairs (Suzy had given him a few new ones by the look of it). 'She was lurking in the lobby, chatting up every man who passed. She nearly got us busted by the vice squad.'

Brad booked out a week later. He came in for one last trim, and left us his business card. 'That's my office in L.A. If you hear anything from Linda, can you e-mail me?'

'Course we will, Brad', I said. 'But you know, she might never come back.' I shouldn't have said it, but the strain of all that secrecy was getting to me – and now Brad was staring at me as if I was guilty of something. I shrugged. 'Maybe she doesn't need a divorce.'

He frowned. 'Maybe Father Nick put her off it. Hey, do you Catholics really believe "Till death us do part"?'

The chop

Macker's beard is not a nice place to be on a Saturday afternoon. But I held my breath and ploughed into it. First, I plastered it in industrial-strength shampoo, which I hoped would finally get rid of that fishy stink. Then Shay rinsed it in scalding water.

'For the love of Jaysus', Macker yelled.

'Shut up! You're Judas, remember?' I waved a canister of hairspray at him, while Shay grabbed his beard.

After Shay had hosed all the suds out of it, I massaged some heavily scented conditioner in.

'But there was no bleedin conditioner in those days', Macker protested.

'Well, it's a modern adaptation', I said. 'Enrico Bendini's going to film it.'

Father Nick had been bragging all over town about the Passion play he was staging in the church grounds on Easter Sunday. *St Ned's Easter Extravaganza* he was calling it on the posters he had put up in all the shop windows.

Mrs O'Toole immediately tore down the one he put in her post office. She was in a snot because she had wanted the part of Mary, but Father Nick had given it to rich Mrs Uberman.

'The Passion play is supposed to be held on Good Friday', she sniffed. 'And who ever heard of a woman playing Our Lord?'

One of Enrico's demands had been that the French actress Sylvie Fouton got to play Christ. 'It will be a dead cert for the Palme d'Or', Father Nick had assured the parish committee, who had eventually agreed to pay Mademoiselle Fouton's 'nominal fee' plus twenty per cent of the box office takings.

That's why the rest of the cast was strictly budget basement: frustrated local actors who were delighted to show off their talent to an audience other than their acting school classmates.

We weren't complaining; Father Nick had appointed us as the official hairstylists to all the cast except Mademoiselle Fouton (she was flying her own stylist over) – and, since Enrico was in a huff about the low budget, he didn't come near us.

'Isn't this great, Shay? We've got complete creative control for a film that's going to be banned by bishops and shown in art-house cinemas all over Europe.'

'Yeah. I wonder if they'll know these beards are really Irish dancers' wigs?'

We had bought the curly wigs from the Leaping Leprechaun dancewear shop, and, since most of them were red, we had dyed them black and artfully bleached in a few grey hairs. Now Shay was weaving one of them onto the trendy goatee of local amateur thespian Conor Doyle – who was sitting there with a scowl on his ungrateful, pimply face.

'Never mind Barabbas; I look like bleedin Rasputin', he was saying.

'Shut up. It'll help your career', I said.

Budget-conscious Sonny O'Toole who, when he's not being a local councillor and an accountant, is the parish treasurer, told a petulant Father Nick that the church funds would not even cover the cost of costumes. So we suggested using only long-haired blokes as Roman soldiers.

'We can put a few old colanders on their heads, pull the hair through some of the holes and fix it with extra-strong gel so it looks like those big rigid brush things the Roman soldiers always had on their helmets', I said.

The only problem was Councillor Mickey. Father Nick had persuaded him to play Pontius Pilate – but he refused to go bald. 'Get away from my feckin head', he said as Shay lunged at him with the electric razor.

'But my Da says the original Pontius Pilate was the first bald celebrity – he became a famous TV cop later and even changed his name to Telly.'

In the end, we used a pair of tan-coloured tights. 'Here, Shay, put the bum of them over his bonce, and tie the legs on the nape of his neck.'

'I look as if I've got a huge carbuncle on the back of my head', Mickey whined.

'Well, if we cut it, the tights'll ladder and you'll look like you've got leprosy', I said.

The Duchess of Straththigh was relishing her role as Mary Magdalen. 'To think that I converted to Catholicism only last year, and already I'm a fallen woman', she was saying as I dyed her hair a rich chestnut. 'Do you think I'll be able to wash this out?'

'Course you will', I said. 'We'll give you a good bleach-up and you'll be fierier than ever.'

Just then, Father Nick came in. 'What's wrong with your face, Father?' I asked. He looked as if he was about to be crucified.

'Bendini has pulled out. He's leaving Ireland. He says the Mick Flick is dead – which is a bit rich coming from a man who specialises in Preek Fleecks for pretentious assholes. Even the trailers need subtitles: "Coming Soon".' He shrugged. 'Well, at least now we can have a male Jesus.'

'Shay'll do it', I said.

'Wha'?' Shay dropped his scissors.

'Well, actually', Father Nick said; 'I was thinking of playing the part myself. Now, I want you to give me a tint to dye for.'

Easter eggs and George Morton just didn't seem to go together. But there he was, looking in the salon window with a smile and a big chocolate egg wrapped in expensive-looking gold tinfoil, with a red lace ribbon. It was after hours as usual; he was obviously trying to avoid our other clients, who were getting curious about Linda's disappearance.

'I'd like to tell him where to put his Easter egg', I said to Shay, but he shhh-ed me. 'Just take the egg – and the money. We need it.'

He was right. Glamourcuts had poached a lot of our middle-class clients. We were left with the celebrities, who spent more time away on film sets or concert tours than in Belgowan, and a few of the native 'old rich' who didn't believe in paying bills quickly (which was probably why they were still wealthy after all these years).

We'd been having arguments over money.

'I'm not bleedin extravagant. This dress costs exactly the same as all your acrylic shirts.'

'Yeah – *all* of them.'

'I thought it was important to blend in with our clients.'

'But do you have to dress like the Duchess? Couldn't you copy Birgitta Stormberg instead? She's made dozens of films without any clothes. Saved the wardrobe department a fortune.'

'Well, she spends it on bleedin cosmetic surgery.'

'OK, then what about Jurassic Rox? They've been wearing those drainpipe jeans since the 'eighties – and they're not a pretty sight.'

In the end, even Shay had to agree that, to be truly a part of the community, at least one of us needed a designer addiction – and shopoholism was the least expensive. We couldn't afford the aftercare that went with a cocaine habit, unlike Steve Oldman who was always flying off to Montana for detox breaks.

We also had to keep up with our neighbours in contributions to charity. Out in Ballyskanger, it would be enough to drop some loose change in a collection box outside the supermarket (to send some hillwalkers away to cheer up people in the Third World – and get the stingy feckers out of the pub). But in Belgowan charity meant spending two hundred euro on a ticket for a banquet (I hate caviar but if eating it means other people won't starve, I'm willing to ignore my taste buds).

So that was why we were already three months in arrears with our mortgage, and the letters from the building society had gone from polite to nasty. I was holding the last one, wishing I could just crumple it up
and throw it in the bin like all the others.

>Dear Mr and Mrs Duffy,
>
>We note from our records that you are more than ninety days overdue in your mortgage repayments and that you have ignored our numerous attempts to contact you by post, telephone, fax and e-mail.
>
>If the arrears are not paid within five working days, we will have no option but to pursue the matter through legal channels.
>
>Yours sincerely,
>Rob Cashin
>Manager

'Shay, will the salon be repossessed?' I tried to hold in the tears as I looked at the row of basins, the chairs and the big chrome scalp-massaging machine which had cost us a fortune.

'I hope not, love.' He kissed the top of my head, then coughed. 'Kay, you'll have to go easy on the hairspray; that stuff's expensive.'

Our salon wasn't the only thing we were losing. A few nights later, we came home early from the pub and saw Mrs O'Toole with a young couple. The three of them were coming out of the door beside the post office; the only thing behind that door was the staircase up to our bedsit. The couple looked like 'non-smoking professionals'; the kind you read about in all those 'accommodation offered' ads on the newsagent's window. They were shaking hands with Mrs O'Toole and getting into a small but brand new car.

As they drove away, Mrs O'Toole stuffed something into her apron. 'Probably a month's deposit', Shay said. He called across the street: 'Hello, Mrs O'Toole.'

She put her hand to her mouth. 'Oh merciful hour! Youse nearly sent me to my maker.'

'He should have given her mother a refund', Shay said under his breath, then shouted across at her: 'What were those people doing in our apartment?'

She put her hands on her apron and smirked. 'They're going to be moving in next week. I was going to give youse notice to quit tomorrow morning – when youse'll be sober.'

Shay put his arms around me. I lay my cheek on his shoulder and looked at Mrs O'Toole. 'You old maggot', was all I could say, and I don't know if she even understood me because it's hard to talk clearly when you're crying. 'You rotten old lump of –'

'What seems to be the problem?' We turned round and looked into the big red face of Sergeant Rory. He was obviously off-duty, because he was wearing only part of his uniform – the shirt and shoes, with a pair of tweed trousers. 'Are you all right, Mrs O'Toole? I hope these two aren't giving you any trouble.'

She clutched her chest. 'My poor old heart's not able for arguments over rent.' She sniffed and scrunched up her face, but her beady eyes were shooting poison arrows at us.

Sergeant Rory put a big knobbly hand each on our shoulders and spun us round to face him. He was turning the colour of a ripe beetroot; his forehead was drenched and great gobs of spittle were spraying our faces. 'If ye ever do anything to upset that nice, decent lady, ye'll answer to me and Judge Penton. Ye can spend tonight packing, and I want ye out of there by tomorrow morning – or I'll charge ye with disturbing the peace. This is a respectable town now; there's no room in it for the likes of ye.'

Shay had to hold me up as we stumbled up the stairs – and it wasn't just the drink this time.

Vidal greeted us with guilty eyes. 'Traitor', Shay said, but he picked him up and hugged him tightly. I hugged the two of them. Vidal licked our tears and whimpered.

'Don't be too hard on yourself, Vidal', I sobbed. 'Go pee on the walls – go on, do a nice big plop on the carpet. We won't be cleaning it up.'

That night, we cried, drank a few six-packs of disgusting cheap beer we kept for emergencies, and finally worked up the energy to carry our bed and sofa down the steep, narrow stairs and a few doors down the street to the salon. They looked strange in the middle of the floor.

'I suppose we could pretend they're modern art', Shay was saying. 'A satirical comment on the casting couch and all that. Our Hollywood clients would appreciate it.'

We felt a bit exposed, sleeping there in full view of passers-by. 'I don't think it's a good idea to have a late lie-in tomorrow morning, love', Shay was saying as I pulled the covers over our faces. Even Vidal was embarrassed; he hid down between our feet. Outside, it had started to rain.

'I suppose we could be worse off', Shay was muttering into my hair. 'I mean, we could be like Linda Morton – dead.'

The salon was going to be repossessed at the end of the month, according to the little worm from the building society who ambushed us as we locked up one night. Meanwhile, we tried to take in as much cash as possible; we needed it for food and the deposit on another bedsit, if we could find one.

We couldn't afford to pay Lorcan but he stayed on anyway. 'My parents give me pocket money – they still think I'm studying architecture at Trinity College', he said. Shay squeezed his shoulders and forced a smile. 'Free haircuts forever – that's all we can give you until we're back on our feet.'

Roz helped out when she could, in between manicuring the occasional client, but it wasn't enough to pay us the rent on her chair, or even her bus fare out from Ballyskanger, so she was leaving at the end of the week to work in a beauty salon in the city centre. 'I'm sorry, Kay', she blubbered, covering my new top in snot. I hugged her.

We left them both in charge while we went to the bank; the manager had sent us a stiff letter demanding a meeting about the state of our current account. We had written a few cheques without finding out whether our balance would cover them; we couldn't check it because the cash dispensing machine had withdrawn our card and we were afraid to approach the stuffy tellers, but we knew that excuse wouldn't impress the manager.

There was the usual pre-lunchtime queue and only one teller. 'Just our luck', I whispered to Shay. 'It's Fintan Stapleton, whose granny got my granny banned from the bingo hall for falsifying the numbers.'

Fintan was very pleased to see us. He smirked until we got to the top of the queue. 'Youse are in the wrong queue. Youse should be outside that door over there.' He nodded towards a brown door marked 'Manager', shaking dandruff all over his navy jacket, and we shuffled over to stand behind at least twenty other people.

None of them looked worried, I noticed. The woman in front of us was clutching a brochure with a picture of palm trees on it. 'Holiday loans', it said.

The manager, Mr Cramp, was squinting at a computer from behind nondescript glasses. He waved to us to sit down in two spongy chairs. I was glad we'd had chicken curry with blackbean sauce from the Chinese take-away the night before; the bank manager wasn't going to be the only person making a stink.

He turned around and frowned at us. He picked up a piece of paper from his desk and handed it to us. Shay took it and we both glanced at it; it was a copy of our statement, with a big red circle around the balance.

He spoke slowly and precisely, as if he had got a hair between his teeth and was trying not to swallow it. 'I'm not going to waste any more of my valuable time talking to you. I only called the pair of you here to make it clear that, as from now, you are not entitled to use our facilities, and we will be taking the matter further. Now that's all I want to say. Get out – get out!' He pointed to the door; I noticed his finger was shaking and his glasses were sliding down his mean little nose (he probably saved on tissues).

I couldn't resist giving him the two-finger salute as we walked out; he had lost the power to do any more harm to us. 'He can't sue us', I said to Shay as we walked out of the bank: 'We've got no assets.'

It was our last night in the salon. We had originally planned to have a party and then set fire to the place, but it would have been 'too final', as Shay put it. 'Anyway, a conviction for arson wouldn't look very dignified beside a white-collar crime such as bankruptcy.'

We had also decided it wouldn't look professional if we sent flyers around to all our celebrity clients, telling them we were closing temporarily owing to financial problems. In any case, we couldn't afford to have flyers printed or even make phone calls from our mobiles (the salon phone had already been cut off).

So we had told no one except Jason and Gary Wu, over a few pints; they refused to let us pay and promised to meet up for drinks sometime in the future, though we wondered when that would be.

Now we were giving Vidal his last hairdo in one of our basins. 'No crying, okay?' Shay made me promise, so I kept my hair around my face to hide the tears. Shay hummed along with the radio but I knew he was only doing it to keep from crying himself.

'You've taken everything out of the till, have you, love?' I asked Shay.

'Yeah – all one hundred and twenty euro of it. Thanks be to Jayz, that woman let us persuade her to go blonde. She didn't seem like the type.'

'Well, why can't Revenue people be sexy? Maybe it will change her life. Anyway, she was so nice, I was feeling guilty that we never filled out that tax form.'

'Don't worry about it, Kay. We probably weren't earning enough. Anyway, according to *Sins on Sunday*, Belgowan is a tax dodgers' haven.'

'Only if you're a rich foreigner.'

We were trying not to talk about our future; it was too depressing. We had turned down Gary Wu's offer to put in a word for us at Glamourcuts, after Shay had seen Vicky making a snipping gesture with her scissors as he was passing by their window. 'It was at crotch height; I'm sure she was thinking about me.'

Anyway, we couldn't take orders from another hairdresser, after six months of being our own bosses. Buying a car and making house calls was another non-runner; the car insurance people obviously thought the under-twenty-five age-group was the richest, judging by the money they wanted.

My sister Bernie had found me a job in a video rental shop out in Ballyskanger Shopping Mall. Shay had a friend who had just been sacked from a petrol station on the Clonbollard dual carriageway and had assured him that the boss would take anyone. We would have to forget about hairdressing for a while.

We couldn't afford to rent another bedsit, even in Ballyskanger; first we needed to pay off the interest on our debts so we could crawl back to Mr Cramp at the bank for another loan.

Meanwhile, Mam had offered me my old bedroom back in Ballyskanger, and had grudgingly agreed to let Shay sleep there too. We would be sharing my old single bed; our double bed wouldn't fit in, so Dad's friend Anto was going to sell it and the sofa at a car boot sale out in Clonbollard.

'Shay', I said at last, 'do you think we'll ever be able to open up a salon again?'

'Course we will, love. This is just a normal set-back. Bigger businesses than ours have gone belly-up, and that hasn't put them off starting up again – all you have to do is change the company name. "Ugly" was probably an unlucky name, anyway; people are sick of irony. Let's call the next salon we open "Gorgeous".' He sang along with the radio: 'You're gorgeous, I'd do anything for you....'

It was quiet on the street outside. The pubs had been closed since half eleven, and, this being an upmarket town, most of the drinkers had gone back to their own homes for a nightcap instead of roaming the streets looking for a fight, the way people did in Ballyskanger.

'How are we ever going to get used to living out there, Shay?'

'We just have to think of it as a temporary situation. We'll be back in Belgowan sooner than it takes to grow-out a bad haircut.'

Belgowan. For most of my life, all I had wished for was to return to my childhood town. I finished putting rollers in Vidal's fur and carried him over to the window. 'Take one last look, pet. You won't have to wear a muzzle on the street in Ballyskanger. You can bite anyone you like and – Vidal!'

He leapt out of my arms and sprinted out the door, which we must have left open. I heard a loud 'Meouwwwl!' and a big marmalade cat ran past. Shay and I ran out after them. 'Vidal! Come back!' we called, but it was no use; they had disappeared round the corner. The last we saw of Vidal that night was a hundred pink rollers flapping on his long henna-coloured coat, and suds flying into the night air. All that was left was a little white splotch of deep-conditioning creme on the pavement.

All night, we worried about him. 'If he's caught without a muzzle, he'll be executed by that poxy dog warden', I cried.

But he came back in the morning with a dead rat in his mouth and a guilty expression in his yellow eyes.

'Oh, look, Shay, isn't he sweet? He's brought us a present.'

Shay made a big show of taking the rat reverently and pretending to put it in a cupboard; Vidal had sulked for a whole night once, when we had binned an old shoe he'd given us.

The bailiffs arrived just as we packed the last of our stuff into Macker's van. It was a tight squeeze, because he had been fishing since dawn, but we supposed a few dead pollock on top of our pillows couldn't make our lives any stinkier.

I'd never seen bailiffs before, but from the stories my granny used to tell, they were men with red faces, rotten teeth, scuffed shoes a size too big and too-tight wedding suits which always had rips on the bums where loyal family dogs had attacked them as they evicted widows and children out of little cottages.

The five standing outside our shop were close enough to her description, but they wore jeans and padded anoraks – which they didn't remove despite the fact that it was a warm June morning. I guessed they weren't taking any chances.

I recognised one of them: Gouger Byrne, whose wife was always having accidents with her iron. 'How's Mrs Byrne these days, Gouger?' I yelled as we passed him. I wasn't afraid of him; he was small and weedy, which probably explained why he could only bully a tiny little woman like Mrs Byrne (even the kids bullied her).

But the guy standing behind Gouger looked as though he could do some real G.B.H., so I picked Vidal up and squeezed onto Shay's lap in the passenger seat of Macker's van.

Out of loyalty, Macker reversed into the bailiffs' pick-up truck. 'Youse can sue me; I'm not insured', he cackled and waved goodbye in fisherman's sign language. 'We ruined their day on them', he told us as he raced off in first gear (it was the only gear the van had). 'They were expecting tears, a fight, broken windows – did youse see the big metal battering ram they had on the back of their truck?'

I looked back at our salon, admiring the yellow paint job we'd done a few weekends before. The tears poured down my cheeks. Shay held me tight; he was crying too. Vidal licked our tears and whimpered. The Cranberries were singing on Macker's radio: 'It was just my imagination, just my imagination...'. Now I felt as if I had imagined having a salon in Belgowan. I clung to Shay – I wasn't going to let him disappear.

'There's George Morton', Macker was saying. 'He's always walking around the back roads these days. He looks lonely, poor devil. I wonder where his wife is.'

'Macker', Shay said suddenly, 'are you missing a fish trap?'

'Well, not that I know of. Missing a few lobsters, though: a bloody big conger eel got into one of my traps and munched his way through everything but the bait. But that's Belgowan for you: even the fish are getting uppity.'

Dandruff

Nothing kills passion faster than the smell of boiled bacon and cabbage from downstairs and the knowledge that your parents, brother, sister and little nephew can hear every amorous sound you make. We tried turning my TV on loud, but that didn't go down well with the family at four a.m.

We were stuffed into my little bed, Shay, Vidal and I, like the proverbial sardines; sandwiched between my parents' room and Starsky's. Bernie slept directly above us, in the attic, with little Robbie in his cot at the end of her bed. She was waiting for Ballyskanger Borough Council to give her a flat, which would take a lifetime, judging by the large number of unemployed single mothers living with their parents in the area.

Meanwhile, she was happy to avail of the free babysitting service. 'Maybe we should open a crèche', I said to Shay as we spent yet another Saturday night rocking Robbie to sleep; Bernie was out pubbing with Fergal. 'Since youse don't have any kids of your own, I'm giving youse a loan of him', she had said as she was getting onto Fergal's motorbike.

'But Bernie', I was yelling, 'Shay and I were going to go to the flicks.' It was too late; she and Fergal had disappeared in a cloud of petrol fumes.

Mam and Dad went off to their line-dancing class or salsa or tae-kwando; they weren't fussy as long as it was a rigid appointment that couldn't be broken. We had come along at the right moment for them, just when they'd grown tired of being doting grandparents. 'We reared the three of youse', Mam said to me. 'We're done rearing. Anyway, it'll be good for you and Shay to practise being parents.'

Our new jobs were minimum-wage dole-queue busters; after the bus fare we barely had enough to buy a pint in the Shaven Head, never mind pay off our debts.

I worked alone during the day and often late at night (those students were always leaving without notice). It was part of a big chain of video shops and, judging by the money I took in, was doing very well. But I had to pay for my uniform – a red acrylic T-shirt with 'Goggle-Eyes Video Rental' stencilled in yellow across the front and back.

I had expected an easy job; what could be nicer than watching videos all day? But the squadron of minimum-wage managers who patrolled the suburbs in company vans was liable to attack at any time of day or night, making sure that I had scrubbed every video cover and, especially, that I hadn't robbed the till.

The videos themselves depressed me: all our ex-clients were starring in them. I even saw an old *Toyboy* video of Linda Morton in which she did impossible things with a hoover and a team of brick-layers (they looked like the Village People but obviously weren't, judging by the things they were doing).

Shay always met me at the end of my shift, even though it meant taking two buses from the petrol station, and we got another bus back to my parents'. But whenever I finished early enough, we caught a late movie in the Cineplex out in Clonbollard, or went into the amusement arcade next door, where we spent our wages on one-armed bandits and those furry toys that always managed to dodge the grabbing device – anything to have some time alone together.

One Saturday, we both had the afternoon off so we bussed down to Belgowan and just walked around in the rain. We felt too sad to call in and see any of our old friends; it would only make life in Ballyskanger unbearable. But we dared each other to look at the shop; we were still hoping no one else had bought it.

It was still empty, with a 'For Sale' sign and the logo of the auctioneer woman next door's firm. 'At least those leeches in the building society haven't made any money out of it yet', I said to Shay as he put his arm around my shoulders. The windows were grimy but we could see that the chrome basins were still there, the chairs, and even the head-massaging machine which looked like an alien in a video I had watched at work that morning.

The cat that Vidal had chased through the town on our last night was sheltering under one of the window ledges. 'Just as well we left Vidal at home', Shay was saying.

It was getting dark. 'Time to go home', I said, and we found ourselves standing across the street from our old flat before we realised that it wasn't 'home' anymore; 'home' was now a small bedroom in my parents' house, in a grey Ballyskanger housing estate, far from the sea air and the celebrities parking their Ferraris outside our salon.

There was a light in our window, behind the new beige curtains; the non-smoking professionals had probably given our *Simpsons* curtains to Oxfam. We could see the couple now – well, their silhouettes – in the backlight. They were embracing, kissing.

'Assholes', Shay said.

'Just what do ye two think you're doing?' We felt a pair of big, sweaty hands on our shoulders and turned around to see Sergeant Rory. 'Spying on respectable people – I could have ye jailed for that.'

'Go ahead and arrest us', I sobbed. 'I'd rather go to jail than move back to Ballyskanger.'

Shay shussh-ed me. 'We didn't mean it', he said to Sergeant Rory. 'It's just that we miss this town so much.'

Sergeant Rory's features softened so he looked less like a beetroot and more like a turnip. 'Off with ye', he said gruffly.

'I suppose it must be boring for him in Belgowan, now we're gone', I said to Shay as we waited at the bus stop. 'I mean, he's only got respectable people in the town now.'

'Well, he could be keeping busy with drug raids on the celebrity mansions', Shay pointed out. 'But I suppose he'd rather not take his chances with all those armed bodyguards.'

Sunday used to be our day for lounging around the bedsit in our PJs, eating a big tub of low-fat ice-cream and listening to our CD collection which dated from our apprenticeship days in the 'nineties. Or, if it was sunny, we used to stuff Vidal into a sports bag and smuggle him down to the harbour to go for a trip on the trawler with Macker; we always carried a muzzle, just in case Sergeant Rory or the dog warden stopped us. It had been fun, being twenty-four and in love and independent of everything and everyone except each other.

But that had been in the old days. Now we were making excuses to Mam if we missed Sunday breakfast, lunch or dinner. We were bartering babysitting for the use of the shower because the immersion tank wasn't big enough for the whole household to have showers the same day (luckily, Starsky never bothered).

Worst of all, we couldn't take a day off whenever we felt like a lie-in. We couldn't stick a 'Closed for Urgent Repairs' notice in the window of the video shop or the petrol station and cancel all our bookings. And we couldn't even call in sick, because minimum-wage employers don't do sick pay schemes.

Anyway Mam would be into our room brandishing a chip pan if we missed a day of work; she needed every cent of the thirty euro a week we paid her for our board and lodging. It was more than Bernie paid out of her unmarried mother's allowance, but at least it was less than we would have to pay a landlord, so we didn't complain.

Mam did, though. 'You and Shay are costing us a fortune in electricity and that dog is eating us out of house and home. And shampoo is very expensive, you know. You should get that hair cut – you're not a hairdresser now.'

I tried not to cry as I sat in the bus, thinking about that last bit. Mam had cut me more than the sharpest scissors could.

But at least I had my Shay; I knew he'd never let me down.

I was going to surprise him and pick him up at work. I'd been so depressed after Mam's comment that I'd persuaded a part-timer to take a few hours at the end of my shift at the video shop. Anyway it was safer for me; he was a big guy, and more capable of frightening off the local thugs who were always hanging around the video shop as I locked up, waiting for the last customer to drive away so they could point a blood-filled syringe at me and get me to empty whatever cash I hadn't lodged in the safe.

The bus wheezed away from me on the dual carriageway, and I pulled up the hood of my rain-jacket. The petrol station was across the road, and a boring middle-of-the-road grey car was parked at the pump. A man with brown-going-grey hair and an off-the-peg grey suit was filling his car and arguing with a child who wanted sweets in the shop inside.

'Your mother said you're not to eat FizzyLizzies – they're full of preservatives', he was saying.

'You ought to fill yourself up with a few preservatives to stop your hair going any greyer', I felt like saying. I don't know why I didn't: after all, I didn't have to be polite to the public these days. There was a kind of free feeling about it; the customers in the video shop came in picking their noses and scratching their bums, so the last thing they expected was politeness. And out there on the dual carriageway, I was just a private citizen coming to meet her husband, who was working in a dead-end job like her own – but was worth a hundred of the cranky man who begrudged his kid a few sweets.

I walked into the shop, looking around for my Shay. There was a guy wearing a green T-shirt with the petrol station logo, younger than Shay and me, awkward-looking. There's a lad who's never had to face a Chamber of Commerce firing squad or bailiffs or bank managers or building society snot-heads, I was thinking, as I watched him nod meekly down at the little woman who was wagging her gigantic red fingernail at him. She was wearing a hybrid between black acrylic pyjamas and a business suit, with platform sandals (six months in Belgowan among the designer-dressed elite had broken me of that habit). She was obviously a lower manager; she was Vicky from Glamourcuts all over again, only with a bad haircut. And this wasn't even a career job. Why didn't the guy just walk out?

Why didn't Shay and I just walk away from all this, go off and bum around some hot country where we could pick fruit and live outdoors?

Because we still had hope, I realised. Our optimism was all we had had to start with, and look how far it had got us (at least temporarily). We could do it again, I was sure. I knew Shay was too; he had often whispered to me in bed: 'Someday we'll be back in Belgowan.'

I pretended to be looking for a magazine as I waited for Shay to come in. He must have gone out for a smoke round the back or something. I eavesdropped on the conversation between the boy and his boss (my hairdresser habits were hard to break).

'Right, that's all I'm saying on the subject. But if I ever find those FizzyLizzies mixed in with the Chocoplops again, I'll be deducting an hour from your pay.'

'I promise I won't forget to separate them again.'

'Apology accepted – hey, you! You over there. The magazines are not for reading.'

I had been skimming through a copy of *U Know Who* ('Ireland's Ritziest Read'). The cover had a picture of Sonny O'Toole and Muriel, with a headline 'Accountant to the stars marries childhood sweetheart in Ireland's glitziest town.' Muriel had a classic Glamourcuts bob (you could tell Vicky had done it because it was as rigid as a cyclist's bum). There was an circular inset of Mrs O'Toole being kissed on each cheek by Father Nick and Sergeant Rory and a caption, 'Mother of the groom out-glams bride'. Councillor Mickey Finn was standing behind them; he and Sonny had obviously decided to forget about political rivalries for the photo opportunity.

Inside, I found a small story about the Morton divorce, with a big picture of Linda in red rubber lingerie (it had obviously been taken in her modelling days) and a quote from Brad, her 'hotshot L.A. attorney': 'My client is taking a break on the advice of her psychoanalyst, to prepare for the gruelling battle over custody of her beloved pet, Cuddles. She has expressly asked not to be contacted by members of the press.' George had 'declined to comment when questioned by our reporter at the gates of the six-million-euro mansion he shared with luscious Linda until her mysterious disappearance earlier this year.'

I turned to face the middle manager woman, who was well into her thirties but still had acne. 'I'm looking for my husband – Shay Duffy. He works here.'

'Oh', she sniffed. 'He walked out this morning – left in the middle of his shift. Poor Donal here had to do extra hours.'

Donal simpered and continued stacking the sweets.

It was nearly midnight when I got home. I had waited at the bus stop outside that petrol station, trying to cover as much of myself as possible with the anorak, but there had been no shelter from the driving rain that stuck my jeans to my shins and soaked my socks. After forty minutes, a double-decker had rattled down the dual carriageway, and I had spent another half-hour crouching in the seat behind the driver's cage, with my hood up to hide my face from the lager louts who were sitting across the aisle from me. Then I had walked up from the bus stop on my own to my parents' house.

It was still raining; I was glad, because I didn't want Mam and Dad to know I'd been crying. They were tough old Dubliners who didn't approve of whimpering adults.

I turned the key but someone was opening the door from the inside. 'Kay, we were worried about you!' Bernie said, pulling me in by the sleeves of my rain jacket. 'Shay is going mental. Dad is driving him around the estate looking for you.'

I didn't tell her Shay had done a runner from work. When he stumbled out of Dad's car and stared in surprise at me in the doorway, I just gave him a hug and said: 'What's all the fuss about? I got the
wrong bus, that's all.'

'I didn't want to tell you until after you'd finished work', he murmured in bed. 'I thought you'd cry and then you wouldn't be able to finish your shift. I was going to tell you when I called to the video shop to pick you up, but you weren't there.'

'Sorry. I had no idea. Look, Shay, let's not tell Mam and Dad, or even Bernie, in case they make a stink about you being unemployed. It will be our secret.'

'Alright, love. Whatever you say; they're your family. Anyway, we're good at keeping secrets. Did you see that article in *U Know Who* magazine about the Mortons?'

'Shay, I wonder if they would pay us for telling them what George told us.'

'Nah. They wouldn't believe us, not with Barbara Burrows and Stephanie Dunne claiming to be Ireland's best celebrity spies.'

Shay would have been working the next day (the petrol station paid an extra fifty cent an hour for Sundays), so we had to pretend his shift had been changed. 'That's grand, son', Dad said (men like Dad always end up calling my Shay 'son'). 'Now you can come to Mass and then you can help me with the wallpapering.'

'Eh, I can't; I've promised to help my own Da lay a carpet.'

'I'll go with you, Shay', I said.

We had no intention of going to Shay's house, of course; we didn't fancy sitting around their kitchen table listening to his parents and Barry squabble about everything from religion to the reason for Barry's hangover.

So naturally we went to Belgowan. This time, we promised each other not to pass by the shop or the bedsit. Instead, we strolled down to the harbour to say hello to Macker.

It wasn't raining, so he was sitting on the little pier mending a wire fish trap which had apparently burst open from the inside. 'A great big octopus squeezed itself in, ate all me bait and grew until it exploded', he was telling a wide-eyed American woman, who kept saying: 'Gee, that's like in a horror movie.'

Macker looked up when our shadows fell across the fish trap. 'Ah, how'ya Kay? How'ya Shay?' The American woman frowned at us; we got the message and obligingly stepped aside while she took a postcard-perfect photo of Macker. Eventually she left and he took off his sou'wester and windcheater, revealing a blonde Mohican and a Guns'n'Roses T-shirt.

'Jaysus, me back is sore from all that posing. She's from some American magazine; they're doing a story about this town on account of all the Hollywood stars living here. By the way, I'm in a fillum meself –'

'Macker', Shay cut him short, 'did you find bones in any of your fish traps?'

Macker rolled his eyes and laughed. 'Did I what? Sure the bones are all I ever find these days. The sea around here is infested with gi-normous predators that get into all me fish traps and devour....'

Shay tried again. 'Human bones, Macker. Did you find anything like that?'

Macker stopped weaving the wires on the trap and stared at Shay. 'You haven't been drinking, son? Or taking drugs?'

He took us home to his wife, Maureen, for a fried bacon-and-egg lunch.

'Macker never eats fish', Maureen told us. 'He gets nightmares about them eating him from the inside.'

After lunch, Macker winked at Maureen and she put on a video. 'This is Macker's film debut', she said. 'He's going to give up fishing as soon as his agent finds him the right role.'

It was a five-minute horror flick made by a local film student. It opened with a shot of Macker's bait box and the kind of non-copyright music you hear in supermarkets and on professional wedding videos. A dark grey conger eel came into focus; it had the evil smile that conger eels always have. It began sinking its fangs into a hand! – no, it was an old gardening glove. Cut to shot of Macker, cackling, with shrimps and lugworms wriggling in his beard, and then the credits came up, ending with: 'Shot on location in Belgowan, by kind permission of Belgowan Chamber of Commerce. Special thanks to Councillor Mickey Finn.'

'Eh, that was interesting, Macker', Shay said. 'Y'know, you could do with a beard-trim.'

Macker's eyes lit up. 'Would youse let me friend make a fillum about it? He could call it *The Chop*.'

I took Monday morning off work, to hold Shay's hand in the dole queue. Bernie's boyfriend, Fergal, was with us. Years of practice had made Fergal an expert on how to get the best out of the social welfare system, and he coached Shay beforehand.

'Wear a shiny tracksuit and don't wash your hair beforehand; you don't want to look as though you can afford shampoo.'

Shay put his arm around me as we joined the queue, which was spilling down the steps of the redbrick Social Welfare office.

'They're not all wearing tracksuits', I pointed out to Fergal.

He winked. 'See your man over there in the cowboy hat?' We followed his gaze to a big guy in a plastic Stetson and black leather waistcoat.

'Well, he's a veteran. He says the only job he's fit for is being a cowboy – but he can't get a visa for America. The social welfare officers have given up; no one will employ him.

'And that woman over there with the long grey hair; she's a witch or a wicken or whatever it is she calls herself these days. She's been queuing here since she came back from Woodstock – my granddad remembers her. I'm telling youse, it takes guts to stand here looking like that.'

I turned to Shay. 'Stick with the tracksuit, love.'

Fergal had one other piece of important advice for Shay before we approached the yawning lady at the hatch. 'Here – have a loan of him', he said, leaning down to pick up little Robbie and hand him to Shay. 'Kids look good in the queue. Robbie, c'mon, son, give us a hand.'

Robbie obligingly wailed. 'I wanna Playstation. There's no Santa and we never go on holidays.'

'Youse should think about getting one of your own', Fergal said. 'The Mickey Money keeps me and Bernie in ciggies and pints.'

The lady on the other side of the reinforced glass was obviously immune to Shay's caring uncle image. She told Shay he might not be entitled to the dole because he had walked out of his job.

'Jayz, if I'd known that, I'd have called the manager a silly cow and got myself fired.'

'Oh, that wouldn't work; we investigate all cases of dismissal.' She looked at his application again. 'I see that you're a qualified hairdresser. I'm sure our job placement officer can find you a job in a salon.' I could see by Shay's expression that visions of Vicky were flashing in front of him.

Fergal helped us drown our sorrows in the pub across the road from the Social Welfare office. The lounge was packed with people in shiny tracksuits, many with children. 'You would have been better off not having worked, ever', Fergal scolded us. 'Why do you think I always wear this plastercast on my arm on Dole Day?'

'That woman said an inspector would call to our "place of residence" to make sure I'm not a bleedin millionaire's son', Shay was saying. 'Wasn't Steve Oldman on the dole in the early days of Jurassic Rox?'

'Yeah', I said. 'But that was before he became a big tax-evading earner.'

We were hoping my mother would be out at her yoga classes or amateur boxing lessons on Friday morning. But she had a sudden urge to babysit Robbie. And Dad called his road-sweeping supervisor to say he had a bad case of the flu; he was eager to finish that wallpapering. I got the impression they wanted some time to themselves – maybe they felt the way we did.

'Dad, I think you should leave the walls the way they are, with the old wallpaper', I said.

'Why, Child of Grace?' he said through gritted teeth as he pasted a diagonal strip of striped wallpaper over the sitting room door.

'Cos that new stuff will look all stripy and wallpapery and...pretentious.'

'Well, I'll tell you what, love; you and Shay can stop staring at the walls and go to your jobs. Shouldn't the two of youse be gone on the bus by now?'

'Eh, we're doing the night shift – both of us.'

Dad was still wallpapering the sitting room when the Social Welfare lady called. In fact, he was taking extra care. And Mam was fussing around the room with a feather duster.

The inspector was a pleasant woman who totally sympathised with
Shay – but she wanted him to do a 'Back to Work' course at the local technical school. 'After that, you can even have a career in telesales.'

That night, we lay in bed and listened to the conversation between my parents downstairs. They had turned down the TV so they could mumble; we heard every word.

'That Shay is a just a waster', Mam was saying.

'Yeah, but he's good enough for our Kay; she's always been lazy and selfish. I can see her walking out of that job in the video shop any day soon.'

'She thinks she's better than the rest of us. She never did want to do an honest day's work. I was scrubbing floors when I was her age.'

'The cheek of them', I sobbed into Shay's chest. 'Mam only scrubbed floors in the Ardnarock hotel for two hours every morning, and that was for bingo money. And Dad was on the dole from the day he left school and Starsky was born till when Councillor Mickey got him that road-sweeping job.'

Shay hugged me. 'Don't listen to them, love. We'll be out of here as soon as I get the dole; we can get rent allowance on a little bedsit and work from home, tax-free. All we need is a sink, a pair of scissors and some shampoo.'

We were woken up the next morning by little Robbie, who toddled into our room. He was pointing at Shay and singing with perfect diction: 'Waster. Waster.' Bernie and Mam followed him in, giggling hysterically.

When they eventually went out of the room, I leapt out of bed, slammed the door and opened the window. 'We need some fresh air, Shay.'

But the air was grey and manky. I stared out at thousands of identical semi-detached houses – a 'No Man's Land where everybody was a nobody', as George Morton would write if he saw it. Trucks rumbled along the motorway. The sea mist and the thump-thump-thump of rock stars' helicopters were only a memory. I closed the window and got back into bed with Shay. He held me close. I pulled the blanket over our faces.

Shay got his dole, but finding a landlord who would accept a Social Welfare rent allowance cheque was harder. The 'Flats to Rent' ads in the local newspaper and in shop windows all had the same message, whether it was a blatant 'No Rent Allowance', 'No Pets', or '€1,500 p.m. + bills'. So we just pretended Shay had found another job, and he came to work with me, except when he was collecting his dole; it wasn't much less than his wage from the petrol station anyway.

Extra-strong fixing gel

We were in the video shop, looking at an old Linda Morton video one night (Shay wanted to see the close-ups of 'eighties hairstyles, though there weren't any head shots as far as I could see) when we saw a familiar face at the counter.

'Gary Wu, fancy seeing you here!' I said. 'Shay, get your eyes off those women for a minute —'

'Hang on, love; this bit is exciting. Aw shite; bleedin censors. Jayz, is that you, Gary?'

'None ovver, mate. Good to see ya after, wha', free monfs?'

I felt tears sting my eyelids; Gary's accent sounded so exotic, out here in Ballyskanger.

Sergeant Rory had told him where he could find us. ''E's fond of the pair of you, at the back of it all, you know. 'E still remembers your wedding. Actually, lots of people miss you. Belgowan is noffing wivvout the two of you. The town seems sort of, well, ungroomed. Even Sniffa Dawg's got long 'air now – it's as if 'e's grown 'is 'air in mourning. Steve Oldman's lost 'is 'air – Vicky tried to perm it and it just broke off. 'E's 'ibernating until it grows back; won't even give interviews to '*Ello*. Oh, by the way, did you know Linda Morton came back?'

I clutched Shay to steady myself, but he was shaking. We stared at Gary, who shrugged. 'Yeah, everyone got a shock when she appeared in the pub. She was wiv Jason – you know, your barrister friend?'

I felt Shay tense even more. Maybe it was because he was worried for Jason's moral welfare; after all, they had been drinking buddies for all those months in Belgowan.

'Oh, before I forget', Gary was saying; 'I came to ask the two of you a big favour. You don't 'ave to give me an answer straight away, but I need to know by Friday because I need to tell my business partner in London. I'd better explain: I've resigned from Glamourcuts. I was only working there to suss out Belgowan, because I'm going to open a salon there. It's going to be part of a big international chain. The fing is, I'm going to be based in the L.A. salon, and, well, I need a manager in Belgowan.'

Now my legs gave up. I fell back against the wall and slid to the floor.

'Kay, are you all right?' Shay was laughing. He pulled me up by the hand. We turned to face Gary.

'Yes!' we said together. I burst into tears and hugged first Shay, then Gary.

'Wow.' Gary was staring at the screen. 'Isn't that Linda Morton?'

'How do you know when you can't see her face?' I asked.

Gary and Shay gave me a pitying look. Then Gary sighed: 'It's the hair: I'd recognise that Brazilian bikini line anywhere.'

We were so happy about moving back to Belgowan and into our own little apartment that we forgot about the Mortons, until Jason came in to see us. We were back in our old salon, watching a team of professional outfitters rip out our old sinks; the new ones would be 'ergonomic', whatever that meant. There would be a new name over the salon, too: 'Gary Wu', printed like his signature. We didn't mind; it would still be our salon.

'How'yas?' Jason said, and we turned around to see the familiar grin. His accent was as comfortably common as ever, but he looked more like a barrister should look, now; the pin-striped suit was obviously tailored and the hair looked flat, as if it spent a lot of time under a wig.

'We'll have to sort out that hair', I laughed as I hugged him. Shay squeezed his shoulder.

'So, youse are back, fair play to yiz.'

'Yeah', Shay said, 'we still can't believe it. The company has even bought the apartment upstairs for us; we're living there, rent free.'

'Oh, yeah, that's a nice pad. It used to be that bank manager's – you know, Mr Cramp?'

We stared at him. 'You're joking', I said, but Jason shook his head. Shay and I looked at each other and burst into laughter. I finally stopped laughing long enough to explain to Jason. 'He must have heard everything we said about him after he froze our account.'

'Well', Jason chuckled, 'Mr Cramp won't be around to see you pay off your debts: the bank fired him because he had too many bad debts and money-laundering clients. These rich people know all the tricks. Sonny O'Toole's accountancy practice is implicated too.'

'Oh', I said. 'Poor Mrs O'Toole.' She might be an old witch but she was still an old neighbour.

But Jason was sniggering. 'She kicked him and Muriel out of the house; they've had to get a mortgage on a cheap little semi out in Clonbollard.'

'Jason', I suddenly interrupted him, 'what's this we hear about you and Linda Morton?'

He grinned. 'Oh, yeah, we've become friends, sort of. She's back living with George, you know.'

Nothing would shock us after this, I realised. I looked at Shay, who shrugged.

Jason ran his fingers through his hair; I noticed he'd had a manicure. 'Brad was the one who told me she was coming back. We became good friends while he was staying here, and I spent a few weeks at his place in L.A. He's doing well for himself. He does nothing but celebrity divorces – causes most of them.' He sighed but he didn't look as if he disapproved.

'Anyway, I came down to his pool one morning and there she was, stretched out on a lilo in a microscopic red bikini – she still looks fantastic, by the way. She's totally changed her hair.'

'Oh?' I looked at Shay, who looked just as hurt as I felt.

'Youse wouldn't recognise her', Jason was going on. 'She's had it cut very short and bleached. She looks more Nordic than Latin now; she told me she needed to change her appearance to put her past behind her. It's amazing the difference a hairstyle makes.'

We nodded.

'She asked me about Belgowan, about George, Macker, her boyfriends – everyone really. She even wanted to know how youse were getting on in the salon. So I told her it wasn't the same now that she was gone and youse had lost the salon. Then she cried a bit.'

I felt like crying. I looked at Shay; he had tears in his eyes too. I made a mental note to book us some psychotherapy with Doctor Freudenstein, to sort out all this post-traumatic memory shite. Either that, or we'd write a song about it; it would help us bond with our celebrity clients.

Jason was going on: 'A week later, I was back here, sitting at the bar in Mental when my mobile rang; it was Brad. He said Linda wanted to call off the divorce, that she still loved George, he was the only man who loved her for her brain and not just her body, he was really fascinating and not a male bimbo, etcetera, etcetera. She only ran off in the first place because George's literary publicist had arranged for that Stephanie Dunne woman to do a magazine feature on George, in *U Know Who* magazine – of course they wanted to include Linda, and the publicist was going to fly her family over from L.A. You know Linda can't stand them? She didn't even want them to know she was there when she was staying with Brad.'

'That Brad's a sly one', I cut in. 'He pretended he didn't know where Linda was.'

'Oh, he didn't know until last month. She had been hiding out in Paris with an ex-boyfriend. Then they had a row – his wife came back –
so she asked Brad to take her in. Actually, Brad's a bit fed up with her now; he spent a lot of time drafting her divorce settlement, and now it's all off. She's always running away and threatening divorce, you know. Anyway, it seems meeting me made her come back just a little faster.' He blushed.

'You're a bleedin hero', Shay said, giving him another squeeze.

I was feeling a twinge of jealousy; why hadn't Linda confided in us? She'd had our mobile numbers, hadn't she? We were, after all, her hairdressers – and, as anyone knows, a hairdresser is a combination of confidante, confessor and psychiatrist. And why had George lied to us? That was unforgiveable, even for a fiction writer. I looked at Jason.

'George told us he had murdered Linda', I said.

Jason sniggered. 'Yeah, he told me too. He told half of Belgowan, but anyone could see he was just depressed and didn't want to admit she had left him. He's not much of a liar for a man who makes his living telling tall stories.'

'We believed him', I sniffed.

'Ah, don't sulk, Kay', Shay said, hugging me. 'It's not as if anyone was murdered.'

I squeezed him back. It was hard to be unhappy for more than five minutes. And Jason's next piece of news put a big smile on both our faces.

'I'm going to have another bash at the local elections', he said.
'I'm running as the candidate against dog muzzling.'

'Lying to your hairdresser is worse than lying to your wife', I scolded George Morton. But I wasn't really cross; I was relieved to know that one of our best clients wasn't a murderer after all – and that he hadn't murdered another of them.

He smiled. 'My most sincere apologies.'

I wagged my scissors at him in the mirror. 'If we had been unprofessional hairdressers, that gossip would have got you arrested. They don't have stylists like us in maximum security prisons, you know.'

'You know what I still can't figure out?' Shay cut in. 'Why did you want us to think you were a murderer?'

George sighed. 'It seemed more...romantic than just admitting my wife had dumped me. I am, after all, a writer of bestselling books about hitmen.' He smiled. 'Image is everything in a town like this.'

Shay gave me a look. I turned to face George in the mirror. 'George, there's no shame in having an unfaithful wife in a celebrity town. Don't you ever read *U Know Who* magazine?'

He shook his head and grinned. 'I'll have to re-educate myself.'

'And you should have confided in us, your hairdressers – not bleedin Doctor Freudenstein.'

'Well, he is a top psychiatrist.'

'Did he cure your depression?'

'No – Linda's coming back did.'

'Well, there you are, then. You could have saved yourself the expense and hassle.'

'And, by the way', Shay added, 'we're a bit annoyed that she didn't trust us enough to tell us she was going to run off.'

'Yeah', I said. 'After all, if she thought we were untrustworthy people, she should never have let us near her hair.'

Just then, I heard a growl. It seemed to be coming from under George's seat, but it didn't sound like our Vidal.

'Cuddles!' George chuckled and leaned down to pat his Rottweiler.

But Cuddles was wrinkling his nose and staring at the kitchen door. His brown eyebrows were knitted together as if he was concentrating on something.

'Jayz, he's meditating', Shay said. 'That's what Mike Oldman's guru does when he's in a deep trance. And he's humming – listen. There must be some negative vibes coming from the kitchen.'

George held Cuddles's collar while Shay went into the kitchen.

'Shay, be careful', I said.

'Ah, Vidal', I heard him laugh. 'Is that why you never liked George?'

He carried our whimpering pet out and brought him over to Cuddles, who was snarling now. 'Now, youse two are going to make friends, right?'

'They look anything but friendly', George cut in.

Shay turned to me. 'Kay, pet Cuddles.'

I was worried about my fingers; that muzzle didn't look as if it was securely fastened. Still, I forced myself to touch Cuddles's quivering head.

Shay nodded at George. 'Now, George, give Vidal a stroke.'

'Ah, I think Cuddles will do that if I don't take him out of here', George laughed, dragging the Rottweiler out of the salon.

We looked down at Vidal, who was cowering under a wash basin.

'A lot of good you are', Shay scolded him.

'Ah, Shay, Vidal's not a coward – are you, Vidal? He's just too well-bred to bite a dog who's wearing a muzzle.'

'I wasn't asking him to bleedin fight – I just thought he'd have learned something from us about how to be nice to bad-humoured clients.'

Christmas Eve was busy for us. There were rock stars to be permed and bleached in time for parties on private jets headed for Miami and St Tropez; Birgitta Stormberg wanted her poodle's fur straightened; Linda Morton wanted her blonde locks dyed dark again; the carol singers all insisted on gold highlights, and our local supermarket Santa wanted extensions put in his beard (he was, after all, hoping to catch the eye of a Hollywood agent).

I was so tired, I needed a break, so I hid in the loo where no one could interrupt me. It got boring after five minutes, so I fiddled around with my pregnancy-testing kit and....

'Shay!'

'What, love?'

'We're going to have a baby!'

'Jayz, Kay, are you sure?'

'Course I'm sure.'

There was a stampede outside the toilet door. I opened it to see all our favourite clients standing outside, with suds, rollers, mêche strips and straightening irons hanging out of their heads. Even Macker was there, with the head-massaging machine attached to his beard, as if he was being attacked by a giant squid.

'Look 'oo's comin across the street', Steve Oldman said suddenly. 'It's Father Nick.'

I clutched Steve. 'Don't tell him. Don't any of youse tell him. Shay and I don't want to do the Baptism Preparation Course with that awful Catholic Lesbian Mothers' group.'

'OK', Steve laughed and everyone echoed him.

Linda Morton appeared in the doorway, with the celebrity gynaecologist Doctor McClone behind her. I noticed he had his hands on her tummy, which wasn't as flat as usual.

She gave me a peck on the cheek (and Shay one on the lips). 'Don't worry', she said. 'I know how to keep a secret.'

◆

Acknowledgement:

Thanks to literary agent Jonathan Williams for his expert advice, encouragement and proof-reading.

About the author

As a roving reporter for mostly tabloid papers, specialising in wacky adventures and strange goings on in rural Ireland, **Geraldine Comiskey** has spent 30-odd years living out of a suitcase and wearing wellies with everything. Some of her most memorable assignments have included "dunker training" in a submerged helicopter with the Royal Marines, boarding a trawler with the Irish Navy in a Force Nine gale, wingwalking over Galway Bay, and getting set on fire by stuntmen in the Wicklow Mountains. She has also worked as a serious reporter for the broadsheet press and in a wide range of "real jobs". She is based in Dublin. Her hobbies include visiting haunted locations, buying silly things in discount stores and getting her hair done.

Contact the author: geraldinecomiskey@gmail.com / X: GerComiskey / Instagram: GerGhostwriter / Facebook: GeraldineComiskey9; also on LinkedIn, TikTok and YouTube.

Website: www.GhostwriterConfidential.com

Books by Geraldine Comiskey:

Adult fiction:

Shampoo & Sympathy
Floozies
Chasing Casanova
Still Life
Skin Deep
The Drop-Out
unRIP

Children's fiction:

Battle of the Birds

Poetry collections:

Life: Poems & Lyrics
Death: A Collection of Poems

Books about Irish culture:

Wacky Eire
Wacky Ireland
Wacky Ireland II – Wackier Ireland
Racy Ireland: The Naughty Bits
The Blow-In: Ian Bailey's fight to clear his name
Cash Kills: The case against untraceable currencies

Floozies

Femmes fatales are fighting back

It's not easy being the only dysfunctional member of a well-balanced family – especially when you're a forty-year-old social pariah with a 'princess complex' and a reputation for 'borrowing' other women's men.

Vain and catty, Frida Carey has always been proud to be what every woman loves to hate and what every man is ashamed to know: a floozy. Now she's losing her looks – and, with them, the allure that used to make her irresistible to Mr Wrong.

And she's not the only one. Ignored in public by their married lovers, bullied out of jobs by 'envious' female colleagues, shunned at weddings and Christenings, mocked by women's magazines, sabotaged by love rivals, floozies are forever under attack.

But they're not going to take it lying down. No longer content to be garden-fence gossip-fodder, watercooler scandal or some married man's dirty little secret, Frida and her friends decide to set up a political party to fight for the rights of loose women everywhere.

Armed with killer fingernails, mascara and five-inch heels, the Floozy Party is ready to declare war on respectability.

♦

Chasing Casanova

Imagine Love Island set in a small Italian town with a bunch of middle-aged misfits...

It's 2000 and there's no such thing as Tinder, so Esmerelda Fox goes looking for love in the country that invented Casanova.

At thirty-four, she's dated more duds than studs in her native Ireland – and she just wants some uncomplicated *amore*.

But nothing is ever simple in the land of opera, fashion and the Mafia. Before she can say "Buonasera", she's got a slutty reputation, a toxic boss and a set of colleagues every bit as eccentric as her UFO-spotting ,Elvis-impersonating family.

Soon, everyone is hunting Fox.

◆

Still Life

Beautiful, spoilt Chloe O'Doolahan is a thorn in the side of every socialite in the affluent Dublin suburb of Belgowan. She refuses to accept her place according to the rules of suburban snobbery – and, at nineteen, being the belle of Belgowan is only a starting point for a fairy-tale life full of endless possibilities...

But the red carpet is whipped from under her when her doting Daddy leaves her mother for a floozy and goes off to sip bubbly on the tax-haven island of Santa Moneta.

Through the gossip pages of the national press, Chloe realises that it's not a bad dream.

Forced to work in an office alongside girls who aren't impressed by her, she spends every lunch break gazing at the masterpieces in the National Gallery. Inspired by their complex beauty, she paints a colourful new life for herself.

But there's a rip in her canvas: a charming and ambitious young man, who is irresistibly drawn to Chloe. Just about to get divorced, 'Dear John' is simply not good enough to be in the picture. Chloe doesn't want to have anything to do with broken marriages– and she *never* takes hand-me-downs.

◆

unRIP

A dead celeb has an image to keep alive.

The last critic to drive the knife into Karina Starr gave her the fame she craved…and the mother of her dreams.

When Karina, the lead singer of a struggling Dublin girl band, is found viciously murdered, she becomes a cult icon. In death, she appears more talented, better-looking, a sweet girl loved by everyone – except her widowed mother, Gloria.

For Karina left a diary in which she accused Gloria of being 'the Mum from Hell. Now the diary is a best-seller and Gloria is the kind of mother any self-respecting rebel would be proud to have.

But Gloria remembers a different daughter to the one portrayed by the newspapers: a girl who inherited her father's savage temper.

Now Gloria is under suspicion, up against the police, press, neighbours, and Karina's fans.

♦

Skin Deep

Beauty is only skin deep…until everybody has it.

Cosmetic surgeon Raffaella Bianchi grew up knowing she was the most beautiful girl in Borgocasino, a little town in the Italian Alps.

But she's never been tempted to sashay down the Milan *Passarella* or join the thousands of Italian girls who fight tooth and manicured fingernail for jobs as TV gameshow hostesses. Having experienced emotional pain, she prefers to help other people with a comforting smile – or a sharp scalpel.

But when the plainest girl in the town tries to commit suicide because she's been bullied, Raffaella realises that the only cure for some people is…beauty. So she offers her services free.

Soon, beauty loses its exclusive appeal, ugliness becomes a precious commodity. Now, Raffaella has made enemies, including the mother of a child beauty pageant princess, a jealous husband whose wife is suddenly very desirable to other men – and a crazed dog-breeder who seeks revenge after Raffaella refuses to make her pug more 'pugly'.

♦

The Drop-Out

Providence Wilde is not the kind of girl you'd expect to find sleeping rough on the streets of Dublin.

After all, not many homeless people get to sleep on the sofa in the VIP room of Dublin's hippest nightclub, maintain their gym membership and go on dates in posh restaurants.

Alienated from her family, she discovers that friends are not forever and "freedom" has a terrible price.

♦

Battle of the Birds by Korg the Crow*

*As told to his human ghostwriter

Korg is the bossiest bird in his community. Respected by ravens, rooks, jackdaws, magpies and his own flock of grey crows, he enjoys being King of the Corvids.

But Korg has enemies: cats, birdwatchers – and a flock of marauding seagulls.
In an action-packed summer, Korg protects his patch, makes friends with the songbirds – and becomes a rock star!

Now Korg is telling his story *(with the help of his human ghostwriter, Geraldine Comiskey)*

♦

Life

Poems & Lyrics

Inspired by dramatic events in her native Ireland, and by life itself, journalist Geraldine Comiskey turned to poetry to tap into the pulse of the turmoil.
What emerged was a collection of word-snapshots ranging from the serious to the satirical, the political to the personal, provoking outrage at injustice – and poking fun where it's badly needed. Most of the subjects are taboo in polite company. Dip into it at your peril – and feel free to disagree.

♦

Death

A collection of poems

Death cannot exist without life. This is the existential and essential truth at the heart of this collection. Irreverent and rebellious, humble and awestruck, drawn from the poet's personal experience and contemporary world affairs, these poems are prisms through which she sees life triumph over death. Themes include the war in Ukraine, Pope Francis's *Pachamama* ritual and the plight of Prince Harry.

♦

Wacky Ireland

A romp through the Emerald Isle

Imagine BBC's *Countryfile* crossed with Channel 4's cult series *Eurotrash - and Father Ted*!

Now imagine it as a book of true stories, from scandalous exposés to charming vignettes of rural life, told by an insider who has travelled the length and breadth of Ireland seeking out the weird, the wacky, the naughty-but-nice and the downright shocking – an outrageous romp through the Emerald Isle, where ancient traditions, strange customs and modern obsessions make lively bedfellows and where people constantly surprise you. Farmers, faith-healers, lovesick bachelors, animal antics, ghosts – this is modern Ireland.

You won't find these stories in the tourism brochures, and this book is not for the easily offended, the ultra-conservative or anyone po-faced.

NEW updated edition includes a list of little-known Holy shrines...chapters on the ancient Fair at Maam Cross, the Goddess Fest at the Gates of Hell, Donald Trump, Ryanair boss Michael O'Leary... more about Loftus Hall, spooks in general, feisty farmers, monster plants, Obama, Elvis, Joe Dolan and the mystery of the Boleyn sisters...an explanation of gaelic terms – and a countryman's guide to "culcher".

♦

Racy Ireland: The Naughty Bits

The Emerald Isle was once proud to be the Isle of Saints and Scholars, but is now a land of sinners and swingers, rural romps, cuddle parties, saucy stunts and sex festivals – even the place names are rude!

In the pages of this cheeky little book, you'll meet hookers and bondage mistresses...love-rats and gigolos...celeb porn-stars and potty-mouthed puppets... naughty neighbours and nudists...gender-benders and even a bisexual bull.

Get ready for a racy ride through the Irish countryside on both sides of the Border, as the author, a tabloid reporter for more than 30 years, goes undie-cover with burlesque artists and strippers, tells what really happened when a well-known broadcaster joined the Mile High Solo Club – and reveals just why a top sexpert believes Irishmen have a lot in common with Bill Clinton.

*Includes a list of rude place names on both sides of the Border!

♦

The Blow-In: Ian Bailey's fight to clear his name

A beautiful victim seeking refuge from her high-society life.

A handsome drop-our with a history of domestic violence. A close-knit community convinced of his guilt.

When Sophie Toscan du Plantier, the wife of a wealthy French film producer, was murdered in her Irish holiday home on a remote Irish peninsula, a local freelance journalist thought he had the 'scoop' that would revive his career.

Instead, he was arrested – and spent thirty years protesting his innocence.

♦

Cash Kills: the case against untraceable currencies

Cash kills people: Oliver Hayes murdered Anne Corcoran for her ATM card. Christy Hanley was beaten to death after he sold his horses. Many others died from injuries inflicted in raids or muggings.

Cash kills freedom: Elizabeth Gill never went out again. Michael McMahon fled his own home.

Cash kills dignity: A nephew dragged his dead uncle to the post office to collect his pension, a granddad was beaten in front of his grandson, and young women were pimped.

Cash kills commerce, communities and civilisation.

Spanning 30 years, these stories are about people whose lives were destroyed for sums ranging from thousands of euro to the price of a pint.

Cash makes everyone vulnerable.

♦

Praise for the Wacky Ireland series:

"This is a riveting, rollicking romp of a read and would make the ideal present, particularly for someone living abroad. It is sure to be a huge seller." **Niamh O'Connor, *Sunday World*.**

"...an eye-popping procession of dodgy faith healers, rural swingers, ghost hunters, GAA [Gaelic sports] players, all of Irish life really. Gifted with a never say die spirit and an uncanny ability to find herself at the center of the wackiest stories, she's an ideal guide to the book's theme and this is one of the most singular books of its kind you're ever likely to read about its subject...Nothing escapes her eagle eye and her prolific pen...Geraldine, in her own inimitable way, covers the vast spectrum of Irish life...not a corner of Ireland goes untouched... the unusual stories crisscross the country." **Cahir O'Doherty, *Irish Central***

"*Wacky Ireland* is unreal, everything you never associated Ireland with. It's especially fun coming from a field reporter who doesn't mind stripping down to a bikini to enter a pothole and take its measurements, or risking a ride with the country's worst driver.... Geraldine is one hell of a storyteller ...Geraldine Comiskey, a journalist with the *Sunday World*, sketches a kaleidoscopic Ireland that is brimming with eccentric folks, eccentric rituals, eccentric gatherings, and some very eccentric animals that she came across in the course of her career as a roving reporter. The book promises to be 'stranger than fiction' and on that count it delivers, for you keep flipping pages to find out just how weirder it can get ...Geraldine's style of narration is casual with loads of cheek thrown in, but never once dull or impassive. It's hard to tell where her professional life ends and her personal begins as she is so consumed being a reporter all the time that you almost envy her (especially if you are a journalist) for getting to go on such interesting assignments, meet oddball folks and be one with them ...*Wacky Ireland* stands for the diversity, and a crazy amalgamation of cultures and philosophies Ireland is yet to be known for ...such an honest, witty, even downright cheesy, account of her country can only come from a person who is completely taken in by it, and can't stop exploring it for everything it is worth..." **Anwesha Mittra, *The Times of India***

"Ireland does seem an odd place indeed from the array of eccentrics and oddballs Comiskey has encountered in the course of her work. Not all are as charming or delightful as they would like to think but you can't help laughing at the naughty farmers, crazy football fans and eccentric racehorse trainers. ***"Books Ireland***

"This updated edition of *Wacky Ireland* features truly unique local stories, as well as an insight into 'Culchure' or culchie culture"
Aura McMenamin, *The Echo*, Tallaght.

Made in the USA
Middletown, DE
23 December 2024